"B-but," Abby stammered, "I thought..."

What had she thought? A renewal of their physical relationship had never occurred to her.

"Thought what, Abby? That you and I could live together platonically?" A cynical smile curved his sensuous mouth and his gray eyes were mocking.

Abby was incapable of stringing a sentence together, her heart still racing from his embrace. Wide-eyed, she stared at Nick, her thoughts in chaos.

"Don't look so surprised, Abby darling. We will have a full and normal marriage, and judging by your reaction to my kiss, you will thoroughly enjoy every second of it. Now get that early night you wanted—you look as if you could use it." And, trailing his finger up to her lips, he added softly but with deadly intent, "And remember, I don't share."

JACQUELINE BAIRD hails from Northeast England. She is married and has two sons. She especially enjoys traveling, and has many more ideas stored away for future novels.

Books by Jacqueline Baird

HARLEQUIN PRESENTS
1079—DARK DESIRING

Don't miss any of our special offers. Write to us at the following address for information on our newest releases.

Harlequin Reader Service
P.O. Box 1397, Buffalo, NY 14240
Canadian address: P.O. Box 603,
Fort Erie, Ont. L2A 5X3

JACQUELINE BAIRD

shattered trust

Harlequin Books

TORONTO • NEW YORK • LONDON
AMSTERDAM • PARIS • SYDNEY • HAMBURG
STOCKHOLM • ATHENS • TOKYO • MILAN

For Lena, my mum.
With love.

Harlequin Presents first edition May 1991
ISBN 0-373-11359-5

Original hardcover edition published in 1990
by Mills & Boon Limited

SHATTERED TRUST

CHAPTER ONE

ST IVES sparkled in the early morning sunlight. The beach, washed clean by the tide, was almost deserted. It was September; the families had left, and the children were back at school.

Abby surreptitiously wiped the tears from her eyes as she skirted an elderly couple happily taking snapshots of the bay. You're a fool, she told herself. Jonathan has only gone to playschool, not left home. A wry smile curved her full lips; if she was like this now, she would be a raving wreck when he started full-time education.

Straightening her shoulders, she quickened her pace, blinking the tears from her eyes. The wind caught at her hair and tossed it haphazardly around her shoulders. She surveyed her windswept reflection in a large black plate-glass window, her glance a cursory one. She had stopped worrying about her looks when her marriage had ended some four years ago. She would never go that road again, dressing, acting, living to please one man. It did not work, in any case—her ex-husband had taught her that. She banished the bitter thought to oblivion, and pushed open the small glass door, gaily painted in gold lettering 'The Hope Gallery'. She had her son, her own business and a small circle of good friends, and her life was her own; she was a very lucky lady . . .

'Need a hanky?'

Abby smiled. 'Too late, I've already made a fool of myself crying all the way home, but a cup of coffee wouldn't go amiss.'

Iris laughed. 'I know just how you feel. I was exactly the same when my two started playschool. It's the first step to letting go, and it hurts. Sit down and pretend you're busy, and I'll make the coffee.'

Abby watched the small figure of the older woman

disappear through a door at the rear of the gallery and, sighing, lowered her long body gracefully into an elegant cream hide swivel-chair. She rested her elbows on the desk in front of her, and propped her head in her hands. Iris had been her salvation the past few years, as well as the best friend a woman could have. At almost twice Abby's age, she was like a mother to her, and a beloved aunty to her son Jonathan.

Abby surveyed her surroundings with an upsurge of pride. The gallery was one long room, divided in the middle by a central staircase that led to her living quarters. The walls were lined with paintings, mostly by local artists, one or two of them Abby's own water-colours. In one corner there was a table displaying bronze sculptures, and in another a small retail section, selling artistic and photographic supplies. She would never become a millionaire, but the business made a very comfortable profit. In summer the tourists bought paintings almost as soon as they were hung, and in the winter her regular clientele of local artists, of which St Ives had more than its fair share, kept her business ticking over. Also in the winter she held some solo exhibitions for several artists, and gradually her gallery was gaining a wider reputation.

Yes, she had a good life, and it was stupid to feel so despondent simply because her son had started playschool. Wryly she acknowledged that that wasn't the real reason for her despondency, but that the memories it had disturbed were the problem: the joy she had felt when her pregnancy had been confirmed; the pain a couple of months later, when, keeping an appointment with her solicitor, she had been informed that her husband was divorcing her for desertion. She had fainted, and Mr Farlow, her lawyer, had guessed immediately what was wrong—not hard to do, as by that time she was five months pregnant. He had suggested her husband be informed straight away so the custody of the forthcoming child could be arranged along with the divorce settlement.

She had called Nick from the lawyer's office, and blurted

out her news. His response was engraved on her mind for all time—'Congratulations, but it is of no interest to me. As far as I'm concerned you are no longer my wife, and if you think I'll up the settlement, forget it. Let me speak to your lawyer.' Numbly she had handed the receiver to Mr Farlow. Even the old man, with all his long years of practice, had not been able to mask his distaste at the ensuing conversation. A short time later Abby had received the degree nisi along with a copy of Nick's official disclaimer of the forthcoming child.

For months Abby had lived in a twilight world, out of touch with reality, the pain a dead weight in her heart, then in the New Year everything had changed. She had been walking down Regent Street, no firm destination in mind, when her attention had been caught by an oil-painting of Cornwall in a shop window. It had brought back memories of happier times. Holidays spent with her parents, and Iris, the local woman who had helped out in the house, and looked after the younger Abby, quite often taking her to her own home, and making her feel part of the family.

The very next day, she had put her apartment in the hands of an estate agent, packed up her belongings, and a few days later had turned up on Iris's doorstep in Trevlyn Cove, seven months pregnant and in tears. Iris had taken her in, comforted and cared for her, and when the time had come for her baby to arrive he'd been born in the back bedroom of Iris's house. Some months later, when the man Iris worked for had retired, and the premises in St Ives put on the market, Abby had taken over the lease on the three-storeyed terrace-house with the double-fronted shop. Since then she had never looked back.

'Here, drink this. You look terrible.'

Abby grimaced, shaking free from the past. 'That bad, huh?'

'Well, maybe I exaggerated a bit; anyone so beautiful couldn't look bad.'

'Oh, Iris, you're great for my morale, even if you are a fibber.' Picking up the coffee-cup, Abby drained it thirstily.

'So, shall we get to work unpacking the order that arrived yesterday?'

The two women worked quietly together, filling the discreetly placed fixture, almost empty after the summer rush, until at a quarter to twelve Iris remarked, 'Go on, get away and meet the young devil. You've been watching the clock all morning. I'll finish up here.'

At nineteen Abby had been on her way to fame and fortune as a fashion model; now, at twenty-five, she was what most men would term 'a knock-out,' tall and full breasted with a tiny waist and long, long legs. She was no longer slim enough to be a model, but her feminine curves, the way she moved, added to a stunningly attractive face, projected a sensuality few men could resist. Delicate brows arched over thick-lashed deep green eyes, and her nose was small and straight above a full-lipped, generously curving mouth, the whole framed by a wild mane of red hair that tumbled down her back in a riot of curls.

Abby was completely oblivious to the admiring glances, her whole attention fixed on the young boy clinging to her hand. An indulgent smile curved her lips. Jonathan, with the fierce independence of a three-year-old, had denied missing her this morning, but she had seen the gleam of joy in his big grey eyes when he had found her waiting for him and her heart had flooded with love.

The wind whipped at her wrap-around cotton skirt, and hastily she grasped the wayward material, but, with her other hand fully occupied, she could do nothing about the red-gold strand of hair almost blinding her. A car horn sounded. She grinned and waved at the departing vehicle. Harry Trevlyn, she noted. He must be on his way to *the* business lunch. Superstitiously she crossed her fingers, and wished him luck. So many people were dependent on the outcome.

'Why didn't Uncle Harry stop, Mummy?' Jonathan tugged at her hand, to claim her full attention.

'He couldn't, darling. He has a very important business meeting, but perhaps you'll see him later,' she consoled her son.

'But who were the people with him? Where are they going?'

'I don't know, I never noticed,' she replied briefly. Long experience had taught her not to go into too much detail, as Jonathan could ask questions till the cows came home.

Later she was to wish she had paid more attention to the occupants of the car . . .

Abby paced the floor of her living-room, a half-full cup of coffee in her hand. What was the matter with her today? She was on edge, apprehensive. She tried to convince herself it was just the outcome of Harry Trevlyn's business meeting that was bothering her, but not very successfully. She felt uneasy. Usually her apartment was a constant source of delight. She had decorated and furnished it herself. The light beige carpet, the rose leather chesterfield and complementary furnishings created a light, airy effect that pleased her artistic eye. She loved the old cast-iron fireplace, framed by long, booklined shelves in natural wood, and the few family antique ornaments dotted around, but today it was not having its usual soothing effect on her. Jonathan was fast asleep in his room—he had gone down for his afternoon nap like a lamb, his unaccustomed morning activities obviously having worn him out. Iris was downstairs looking after the gallery. Everything was going smoothly, so why did she feel threatened . . .?

The phone ringing jangled her taut nerves, and, dashing across the room, she placed her cup on the small occasional table and picked up the telephone receiver.

'The Hope——' was as far as she got.

As she listened intently, a slow smile spread across her lovely face. 'That's marvellous, absolutely fantastic!' she opined, her voice rising an octave with enthusiasm. 'Yes, yes, I will be ready,' she promised, then, dropping the phone, she dashed down the stairs shouting, 'Iris! Iris!' She caught her friend around the waist and did a wild jig around the gallery with her. 'That was Harry Trevlyn. It's all arranged. His business lunch was a roaring success. The agent didn't arrive, but the boss of the consortium in person did, and . . .' she stopped for breath ' . . . not only did they look over the site for the Trevlyn Holiday Complex, but they agreed in principle to all of Harry's conditions, and will invest the lion's share of the money.'

'I can't believe it!' Iris cried.

'Trevlyn Cove is saved,' Abby assured her, then, catching the hint of moisture in her friends's eyes, she added softly, 'Why, Iris, I do believe you're crying.'

'Oh, you can't know how good it makes me feel. I've lived there all my life. My Tom worked at the mine till he died, and I was so afraid the village was going to die too . . .'

Abby knew how she felt. Trevlyn Cove—a misnomer, really, as the village was about a mile inland—had been Abby's refuge after her divorce. The people who lived there were her friends and, though her home was now in St Ives, the small village held a very special place in her heart. It was a tiny, picturesque old closed village, attached to the Trevlyn Tin Mine, the only privately owned tin mine still in operation in the country, but which was unfortunately scheduled to close in a few months. The village consisted of two rows of stone cottages, a church and a pub, the whole overlooked by Trevlyn Manor. Harry Trevlyn, the owner, also owned most of the land for miles around. It had been in his family for generations, and he was fighting to make sure it stayed that way for the benefit of his two sons, Michael and David, along with the rest of the small community.

Harry, a widower in his early fifties, had called to tell Abby he had clinched a deal that would ensure new employment for his soon-to-be-redundant miners, and to invite her out for a celebratory dinner with his new business partner.

That evening Abby applied her make-up with care, then, standing up, she crossed to the bed and picked up the dress she had decided to wear—a relic from her modelling days. She slipped it over her head and smoothed it down over her hips. It was cream silk, draped from a halter down over her breasts in a deep V almost to her waist, the back non-existent. A narrow band fitted snugly around her small waist, the skirt hugging her slender hips to fall straight to just below her knee, and a tiny fan pleat at the back enabled her to walk freely. She chewed the corner of her mouth with some dismay as she surveyed her image in the cheval-glass. She had forgotten she had a lot more chest now than she'd had five years ago. The plunging neckline precluded wearing a bra, and she had a nasty feeling that if she moved too quickly she might fall out of it. Still, Harry had said, 'Knock 'em dead,' so why not?

She brushed her hair until it shone like beaten gold, then briskly clipped one side back with a large gilt comb, and left the rest to fall in a riot of curls over one shoulder. Not her usual image at all, but glamour was the order of the evening. Slipping her feet into a pair of high-heeled bronze strappy sandals, she straightened up, and, picking up an almost-empty bottle of Opium, another relic of the past, she dabbed the last few drops behind her ears and down her cleavage. Then, with a saucy wink at her reflection, she grabbed her matching clutch-bag and hurried downstairs.

'Wow, Mum, you look smashing!'

'Thank you, darling.' She smiled, tumbling the dark curls of her son's head with a gentle hand. 'And you have to promise to be a good boy for Aunty Iris, right?'

'I'm always good.' Huge grey eyes twinkled mischievously up at her, daring her to deny it.

For a second Abby was struck by how very like his father he was, but did not have time to dwell on the thought, as Harry and, surprisingly, Michael arrived.

'My God, Abby, you're some woman. I don't know if I dare let my dad go out with you in that dress; his heart won't stand the strain at his age.'

A gruffer voice chipped in. 'Cheeky devil. You'd better watch it or I won't let you have the car.'

'So that's why he's here.' Abby grinned up at Harry, understanding his son's presence. 'He is our chauffeur for the evening, I presume.'

'You don't mind, do you? But I had quite a few drinks at

lunchtime, and I'll have to have a couple tonight to be sociable. Besides,' Harry added, shooting a wicked glance at the younger man, 'he can do his courting better in the BMW than he can in the old Land Rover. Isn't that right, son?'

Michael, with his light skin and ginger hair, could not disguise the blush that ran up his cheeks, and they all burst out laughing.

Comfortably seated in the back seat of the car, Abby felt a pleasant twinge of excitement, her earlier unease completely forgotten. They were going to the Cove Country House Hotel, a place with a national reputation for good food and excellent service, added to which the couple who owned it were friends of theirs. Harry told her that the couple they were dining with had booked in for the night, and the meal was to be their treat, a celebration to confirm the deal. It promised to be a pleasant evening, Abby thought, fondly eyeing the two men in front of her.

Then Harry turned round in his seat and eyed her rather warily.

'Just one thing—I—I told them you were my fiancée.'

The car swerved as Michael hooted with laughter. 'Oh, Dad, what on earth for? You're old enough to be her father.'

Abby was too astonished to make any comment.

'I know that!' Harry snapped with obvious irritation. 'But that Kardis chap got my back up. He suggested I bring my wife, and when I told him I was a widower he said, "I'm sure you don't live like a monk, if the luscious lady you waved to this morning is anything to go by. Bring your mistress." I wouldn't mind betting that's what his secretary is to him—these foreign fellows are like that. You do understand, Abby? I had to protect your reputation.'

Abby was too shocked to answer. The name Kardis had knocked all the breath from her body. It echoed and ricocheted in her brain, almost exploding her mind. It couldn't be . . . It wasn't possible . . . But she was horribly afraid it was . . .

'Abby? Abby, are you all right? You've gone pale. I didn't mean it seriously. I—I just thought—well, hell, a man of my age can't say he has a girlfriend. Fiancée sounds much better, and it is only for tonight.'

Abby dug her fingers into her palms in an effort to control her trembling, and finally managed to speak. 'Did you say the man's name was Kardis? Is he Nick Kardis?' she ground out between clenched teeth.

'Yes,' Harry affirmed with relief, as he realised she was not bothered about the engagement bit. 'He's the boss of Troy International. He was in London, so he came to see the place for himself, instead of sending his agent. A lucky break for me,' he opined happily.

But Abby felt no such luck. Her ex-husband was here, and in a few minutes she would have to face him. How had she not realised? She racked her brains, sure Harry had never mentioned the name of the consortium before, and now it was too late. Her earlier apprehension suddenly made perfect sense. She should have followed her own intuition, she thought helplessly. Breathing deeply, she tried to fight down the rising tide of hysteria threatening to overwhelm her, but it was no good.

'Stop the car!' she cried, panic-stricken, and, leaning forward, she grabbed Michael's shoulder.

'Hell!' he exclaimed, slamming on the brakes, and, pulling into the side of the road, he turned around. 'What the hell was that for? I know Dad's no oil-painting, but you're only going to be engaged for a night. There is no one else, so what's the problem?' he demanded, quite shaken by her hasty action.

'No, you don't understand. I don't mind the fiancée thing—it was very gallant of you, Harry.' Abby managed a rather strained smile, the panic gradually receding. There was no easy way of saying it. 'Nick Kardis is my ex-husband.'

The reaction she got was not what she had expected.

'So?' Michael shrugged. 'People get divorced every day. It's no big deal. You told me your divorce was very civilised. The man gave you sole custody of Jonathan and never bothered you. He seems like a reasonable guy. Why should meeting him tonight be a problem?'

Why indeed? Abby asked herself. With the callousness of youth Michael had described her situation perfectly. Nick meant nothing to her now. All her love for him had died long ago, hadn't it? The denial of his own child had shown her what a heartless bastard he was, and cured her once and for all. Michael was absolutely right. There was no reason why she shouldn't have dinner with the man. The past was finished, dead. She sat up straighter in the seat, her head high, unconsciously jutting her chin.

'You're right, Michael. It was the surprise of hearing his name so unexpectedly, that's all. Drive on, or we'll be late.'

Harry gave her a searching look. 'Are you sure, Abby?' he asked softly as the car moved on.

She reached over and patted his weathered cheek. 'I'm sure, and with you as my fiancé Nick won't even mention the past. We were married for such a short time, he's probably forgotten all about me.'

'I don't believe that for a minute. You are a very lovely woman, but I can't see you with him, somehow. A hard businessman, but a bit of a playboy, I reckon. Not your type at all,' Harry decided with a shake of his head, the matter obviously settled to his satisfaction.

Walking into the foyer of the hotel, Abby was grateful for the firm touch of Harry's hand at her elbow. Thank God he had mentioned the name of their dinner companion, she thought, or otherwise she would probably have taken one look at Nick and passed out at his feet. As it was, her legs were none too steady, but, oddly, inside she felt quite calm, or else she was in shock, she told herself drily.

'You sly pair!' a heavily accented voice exclaimed. It was Antonio, the Italian proprietor, approaching them, with his wife Maria only a step behind.

'We have just heard the news. When is the wedding to be?' Maria asked, grinning all over her face.

'How did you know?' Harry spluttered, floored by the other couple's greeting.

'Mr Kardis told me to show Mr Trevlyn and his fiancée into the cocktail lounge when they arrived. You might have given me a hint, Abby—we are your friends.'

Abby was stunned. She wanted to laugh—the whole evening was speedily developing all the characteristics of a Whitehall farce, but before she could form the words to correct the false information Harry was urging her through into the lounge.

'Later, later, Antonio,' he muttered, striding past the little man.

It took all Abby's self-control not to turn tail and run as her eyes fell on the couple standing at the bar. Nick Kardis. There was no mistaking his wide-shouldered, lithe frame exuding the same blatant aura of raw masculinity that had so beguiled her years ago. Fixing a bright smile on her face, she avoided looking at him, and instead turned her attention to the woman hanging on her ex-husband's arm. Melanie . . . Abby wasn't surprised, but she was pleased to notice that the older woman was, and she felt a flash of pity for her. At the same time Melanie's presence was just the incentive she needed to remain in control of her emotions. Nick's secretary had been his mistress before, during and after Abby's marriage to him. Obviously some things never changed, she thought wryly.

'Abby, this is a surprise,' Melanie twittered.

'Melanie,' she acknowledged politely as in her peripheral vision she noted the two men shake hands.

'Trevlyn. Glad you could make it.' His voice was just the same, deep and throaty. 'And Abby, you're looking more beautiful than ever, my dear,' Nick opined, turning to stand directly in front of her so she had no choice but to acknowledge him. He was angry; she caught the brief glimpse of burning rage before his grey eyes iced over.

'Hello, Nick.' Abby was proud of her cool greeting, and fiercely glad she had dressed up for the occasion. She knew she was looking her best. She did not offer her hand, but Nick took it anyway. Trust him, she thought cynically. The social niceties must be observed, even when he was stabbing someone in the back. His hand grasp was firm and lasted longer than necessary as he insolently allowed his gaze to travel over her in a blatant sexual appraisal, lingering on her full breast for a moment, before returning to her face. She took a deep breath and casually withdrew her hand from his. My God, he had some ego if he thought he could embarrass her at a glance. Years ago she would have blushed at such a studied sensual insult, but not any more. She was now a sophisticated businesswoman, not a stupidly adoring wife.

Abby arched one perfectly shaped eyebrow, and mockingly returned the favour. His six-feet-plus frame was elegantly clad in an immaculate dark blue dinner-suit. He appeared quite a bit slimmer than she remembered. He had always been a handsome devil, and still was, but now his black hair was liberally sprinkled with grey, the grooves from nose to mouth deeply etched. He would be forty next birthday, and he looked every inch of it. Abby hid her surprise by turning to Melanie.

'It's nice to see you again, Melanie. Are you still working or is this a holiday?'

Before Melanie had a chance to reply, Nick interrupted. 'Melanie is my secretary, and this is no holiday, for either of us.'

Why so adamant? Abby wondered; she had only been making idle conversation. Poor Melanie—the same age as her boss, she was fighting a losing battle with the tiny lines around her eyes and mouth. She was still beautiful, small and dark, but her once voluptuous figure was showing definite signs of spreading that the blouson style of her dress could not quite disguise. What a waste, Abby thought sadly. The years Melanie had allowed Nick to use her. Thank God she had escaped that trap and was her own woman now.

'Of course, I should have known,' Abby rather belatedly responded, and, bestowing a brilliant smile on Harry, she asked, 'I'm thirsty, darling. Will you get my usual, please?'

'Allow me,' Nick drawled. 'I'm in the chair. G and T, isn't it?'

'Oh, no—Abby never drinks spirits. A glass of white wine is her tipple.'

Abby could barely suppress her grin. Harry could not have done better if they had rehearsed it. She noted the angry tightening of Nick's mouth and felt a fierce stab of pleasure. He would soon realise she was not the same young girl who had begged for his love. In fact, tonight might not prove as traumatic as she had thought, so long as she kept her cool.

'So your tastes have changed, Abby,' Nick drawled mockingly, deliberately flicking a glance at Harry. 'In everything, it seems.'

'Yes, they have,' she purred. 'When I knew you, I was a teenager trying to act the sophisticate. Now I no longer need to act a part.' Nick didn't like that. His dark eyes narrowed angrily before he abruptly turned to the barman and ordered the drinks.

'This is a coincidence.' Melanie finally spoke. 'I never expected to see you here, Abby, in this backwater. I thought you would have returned to modelling ages ago. Perhaps you're a bit large for a model now; is that the problem?'

Bitch! Abby thought, but let it pass. She had no interest in engaging in a slanging match, and her confidence rose another notch as she recognised her own maturity.

'I had a few offers to return to the modelling world, but I wanted more of a challenge, so I started my own business. You must come and see my gallery some time. I'm sure you'd enjoy it.'

'Selling pictures for the tourists; how quaint.' Melanie laughed derisively.

Abby stiffened at the slur on her hard-won independence. She did not need to look at Nick to be aware of his long body lounging negligently against the bar, listening to the exchange with undisguised amusement. There was no way she was going to let these two jet-setters belittle her, she thought angrily, but there was no sign of anger in her voice when she replied.

'Yes. Why not? In the summer it is a very lucrative trade, but in the off season I present quite a few solo exhibitions. Some by local artists, and some by internationally renowned ones. Ian Harkness, a well known Fellow of The Royal Academy, has had two very successful showings at my gallery, and another is scheduled for December. We are gradually gaining quite a far-reaching reputation.' She didn't add that Ian was a personal friend of hers. She knew Melanie was the type to be impressed by a bit of name-dropping.

'Your drink,' Nick intervened, handing her a long-stemmed glass of white wine. His fingers deliberately brushed hers, and she flashed him a cold glance.

'Thank you.' Was he trying to flirt with her? Calmly she raised her glass and sipped the fine wine, her gaze unwavering on his handsome face. She watched with glee his dark brows draw together in a frown, and his hand shook as he took a hasty swallow of his drink and swung his attention back to Harry.

Abby was amazed at her own poise, elated that his touch had no effect on her.

'Well, this is pleasant, Trevlyn. I had no idea your fiancée would turn out to be my ex-wife. Abby did tell you we were married once?' Nick asked in mock concern.

If she had not, Nick was making damn sure Harry knew now, Abby fumed silently. He certainly was not averse to trying to make trouble for her, that much was obvious. But why was he doing it? She had been the injured party in the divorce, not Nick.

'Oh, yes. Abby told me all about her brief marriage. She was far too young, of course. I never believed in teenage marriages myself; a man should have more sense. I'm always telling my sons that.'

Abby almost choked on her drink at the look of pure rage on Nick's face, and Harry, bless him, rambled on quite happily, completely oblivious to the implied insult he had handed out.

'You were jolly civilised about the divorce; I admire you for that. It must have been hard to give Abby sole custody of the boy, but very wise. It makes it much easier for the child to accept a new father if there are no comparisons to be made. Jonathan is a fine fellow, you need have no fears about his future.'

Nick could barely contain his anger, and Abby was struggling to contain her amusement. It did her heart good to see the great Nick Kardis on the receiving end of an insult for a change. He drained his glass in one gulp and slammed it down on the bar; she was surprised it hadn't smashed to smithereens.

'Yes, I'm sure you're right,' Nick agreed, and, with an abrupt change of subject, added, 'I think our table is ready; shall we go through?'

A broad wink from her so-called fiancé told Abby that Harry was a lot more intuitive than he appeared on the surface, and at that moment she could have hugged him. Unfortunately she did not get the chance. Nick grabbed her firmly by the arm, holding her back so the other two preceded them out of the room.

'He thinks I'm the father of your child. Wasn't that a bit cheeky of you, my dear Abby?' he grated sarcastically.

'I don't know what you mean, and let go of my arm,' Abby demanded icily. His long fingers, curved around the bare flesh of her upper arm, had set off a nervous trembling in her stomach, and she had a sinking feeling that she might have been just a bit overconfident. Virtually on her own with him, she felt much more threatened than when Harry's solid bulk had been there to protect her.

'I'd like to break your bloody neck,' he murmured, bending his head to hers, a patently false smile twisting his hard mouth.

Abby shivered beneath the icy anger in his steel-grey eyes. She had no idea what he was so furious about, and she had no chance to find out, as

Melanie had stopped in the doorway, and called back in a demanding voice, 'Come along, Nick, darling. I'm starving.'

CHAPTER TWO

ABBY breathed a sigh of relief as she sat down at the table. Harry had taken the place next to her, and for that she was grateful. Although Nick no longer meant anything to her, she preferred to be as far away from him as possible.

Antonio presented the menu, and declared, 'As this is a celebration, allow me to provide champagne on the house.' She fought back a grin as Harry, gracefully if a bit warily, accepted. It was obvious he was not very sure just what celebration Antonio was referring to—the success of the business venture, or the fake engagement. The men ordered the meal, and Antonio, with an exaggerated flourish, opened a bottle of vintage champagne, pouring the sparkling wine into fluted crystal glasses.

Raising his glass and touching it lightly to Abby's, Harry said suavely, 'The toast is to us.' His benevolent smile encompassed the whole company, while adroitly avoiding the reason for the celebration. Nick Kardis had no such reservations, and Abby immediately had second thoughts about the seating arrangements as she raised her head, her green eyes clashing with predatory grey ones.

'Have you two been engaged long?' Nick enquired silkily, adding, 'I couldn't help noticing you are not wearing a ring, Abby.'

Trust him, she thought bitterly; he never misses a trick.

Plastering a patently false smile on her face, she responded sweetly, 'Not long, but I didn't want a ring, and Harry agreed with me. He is so totally honest, his promise is more than enough.' She knew Nick had understood her hidden jibe; she could sense the tension in him, and, exulting in his discomfort, she could not resist the temptation to expound on her theme.

'It has been my experience that most men give jewellery to women to ease their guilty consciences. Don't you agree,

21

Melanie?' she asked pointedly, allowing her gaze to linger on the rather ostentatious diamond necklace the other woman was wearing. Abby had no doubt that Nick had bought it for his secretary, and the woman deserved it, considering how he used her.

'Lucky Harry. You are going to be a very inexpensive wife,' Nick responded mockingly. 'You certainly have changed, Abby. I seem to remember when we were married you delighted in the jewellery I gave you, and showed your gratitude most enthusiastically.'

Abby paled, then was helpless to stop the colour running up her throat. A vivid memory of Nick giving her a diamond ring flashed in her mind. She saw herself asking how she could thank him, and remembered his throaty response, show me—and she had. Slipping his jacket off his broad shoulders, slowly unbuttoning his shirt, and eventually undressing him completely, she had worshipped the perfect symmetry of his hard-muscled body. She shook her head to dispel the image, fighting down the surge of warmth that the thought evoked. She hated him and what he had done to her. The days were past when a mere look from those grey eyes could light a sexual fire in her which only he had been able to assuage.

'You look flushed, Abby. Too hot in here for you?' Nick queried softly. The magnetic pull of the man had not receded one iota in the intervening years. He knew exactly what she had been thinking.

'No,' she denied hastily, but his eyes caught and held hers, and she was incapable of breaking the contact. There was no denying the spark of physical awareness that flashed between them. The pop of a champagne cork snapped the thread of sexual tension, and Abby swiftly dropped her head to stare blankly at the white tablecloth.

The chemistry was still there, but, Abby told herself, now she could see it for what it was. Lust, plain, old-fashioned lust. What a shame she had not recognised it as such years ago, and saved herself a lot of pain. Suddenly she did not feel quite so confident of her ability to get through the evening unscathed.

The food was served, and she tried to relax, but it was an uphill struggle. She barely tasted the stuffed mushrooms cooked in garlic butter, and it was an effort to swallow the pheasant that followed. Nick, for some reason she could not fathom, was making no effort to disguise his obvious interest in her. The conversation was centred on the business venture, and Abby thankfully let it flow over her, but she could feel his cold grey eyes boring into her, demanding her attention.

Abby, with great self-control, kept her eyes firmly fixed on the plate in front of her, as though she had not seen food for a month. She hated him . . . Nick Kardis, the millionaire businessman with the morals and habits of an alley-cat. Oh, how she hated him! she silently fumed. The force of her feelings had her gripping her fork until her knuckles turned white with the pressure. She had reverted to her maiden name after the divorce, and when her son was born had registered him as Jonathan Kardis Jones, and immediately afterwards wished she had excluded the 'Kardis' altogether.

'More champagne, Abby?' the hateful voice enquired silkily. Raising her head, she quickly covered the top of her glass with her hand. 'Not for me, thank you,' she refused, not bothering to mask the dislike shining in her eyes.

'That's not like you, dear—you used to enjoy a drink. Another glass won't hurt. I seem to remember drink had a most amiable effect on you,' Nick drawled mockingly, his gaze straying to the deep V of her dress, and lingering on the exposed curve of her breasts, before returning to her face.

'No, thank you,' Abby repeated curtly, ignoring his blatant sexual insult. She knew what he was referring to, and hated him all the more. When their marriage had fallen apart, she had been left on her own most evenings, while he'd wined and dined his lady-friends, and she had often had a G and T. Until one night he had returned late, and Abby, her pride crushed, had asked him to go to bed with her. She would never forget his comment—'I don't go to bed with drunks, my dear.' She had never touched a drop of spirits since.

Outwardly Abby was managing to maintain the appearance of a cool, mature woman, but inwardly she felt the first flutterings of real fear curl her stomach. Why was Nick deliberately needling her? She meant nothing to him, and yet he had been simmering with anger all night. Could it be because he thought she was engaged? No . . . he was heartless and immoral, and his faults were too numerous to count, but petty jealousy was not one of them. So why? She had automatically assumed their meeting again tonight was pure coincidence, but now she began to wonder . . .

'Abby.'

Her head shot up as she realised Harry was addressing her.

'I asked if you wanted coffee, love.'

'Yes, please,' she responded, really looking at Harry for the first time in ages. His blue eyes were shining too brightly. She frowned, catching sight of the three champagne corks lying on the table; she had been so involved in her own thoughts that she had not noticed the speed at which Nick had refilled the glasses. She shot him a furious look and his hard mouth twisted in a knowing smile. It was obvious he had not done much drinking, but the other two were both glassy-eyed.

Abby sat up straighter in her seat, her green eyes hard as emeralds. While she had been concentrating all her energy on just getting through the evening, Nick had plied Harry with drink and loosened his tongue. Belatedly she tuned in to the conversation. To her horror, she realised Harry had reached the stage where he imagined Nick was his friend for life, and was becoming quite maudlin.

'You know, Nick, old man, when I first met you I knew, I just knew you reminded me of someone, but I could not think who. I can't believe I was so blind. Young Jonathan is the absolute image of you, like two peas in a pod—yes, you could have spat him out.'

Abby wanted to curl up and vanish; any minute now Harry would let slip that they were not really engaged. Desperately racking her brain for some way to change the conversation, she was saved by Melanie. The restaurant boasted a postage-stamp dance-floor, and a trio to supply the music. Melanie, grasping Nick's arm, smiled seductively up at him.

'Nickie, darling, let's dance.'

Abby breathed a sigh of relief, a smile twitching her generous mouth. Nickie——he hated being called that. But her grin vanished as, with a speed she couldn't believe, she found herself almost dragged from her chair, one large, tanned hand firmly clasping her own.

'Good idea, Melanie, but we cannot neglect our guests. I'm sure Harry would love to dance with you.'

Before Abby knew what had happened she found herself in the middle of the dance-floor with Nick's arms closing around her. She took one deep, controlling breath and managed to bite back the adamant refusal she wanted to utter. With his conceit, he would take it as a challenge, and she had no desire to give him any encouragement. Schooling her features into a polite mask, she held herself stiffly in his arms, refusing to recognise the familiar warmth of his body.

'For God's sake, relax, Abby!' he commanded bluntly. 'I'm not about to rape you in the middle of the dance-floor.'

'I didn't think you were!' she snapped back.

'Good,' he drawled mockingly. 'I thought for a moment you were afraid of me.' And, trapping her hand with his own firmly against his muscular chest, he slid his other arm around her waist and drew her into the inevitable body contact.

She shivered as his hand stroked up her naked back in a lazy caress. The muscular hardness of his thighs moving seductively against her made her shockingly aware of his potent masculinity. For a second she almost succumbed to the sensual invitation his body was offering, then sanity prevailed. She tried to wriggle free of his provocative hold, but he easily restrained her. Chuckling, he murmured throatily against her ear.

It's so good to hold you in my arms again, Abby. We

always fitted together so perfectly. God, but I've missed you.'

The colossal nerve of the man took her breath away, and she just restrained herself from kicking him in the shin. 'Don't bother, Nick. I've heard it all before. This is Abby, remember? I know what a liar you are, so save the sweet talk for your lady-friends, hmm?' she prompted cynically.

A look of surprise flashed in his grey eyes, but quickly disappeared as he moved his head to study her expression.

'If we are talking about liars, Abby dear, surely you must take the Oscar?' he sneered, tightening his grip on her waist. 'Tell me, what would your estimable fiancé say if I told him the son you claim is your ex-husband's is in reality the child of some man you picked up before you were even divorced?'

'You're incredible,' Abby snorted in disgust, ignoring his question. 'You even lie to yourself. Is that how you salve your conscience? Don't bother to answer, I'm really not interested,' she concluded, catching sight of Michael entering the restaurant. She just wanted to leave. 'Excuse me,' she murmured, and endeavoured to ease out of Nick's arms, but he pulled her closer to him.

'Now, wait a minute!' The demand was harsh and edged with anger. 'If anyone's conscience needs salving round here, it's yours. My God, you certainly had me fooled. I owe you and your child nothing.'

Abby paled beneath the icy contempt in his grey eyes. She could feel his fingers digging into her waist, and she had a nasty feeling that he would have preferred it to be her neck. Then suddenly it hit her. She knew why he had been so angry all evening, of course—the money. A smile tugged at the corner of her mouth, but she repressed it. She was going to enjoy this.

'What do you mean?' she queried with fake innocence.

'Oh, come on, Abby. I gave you a very hefty divorce settlement by anyone's standards. You should be flattered you're the only person who has ever outsmarted me. The one thing I can't understand is why you bother working—you certainly can't need the money, unless

Harkness took you for the money as well as a fool,' he opined cynically.

Abby did not understand his reference to Ian Harkness, and wasn't about to ask, but the rest was very clear. She gave a small laugh. 'I see you want to know what happened to your money. Why? Did you think I would behave like some romantic heroine in a novel and refuse to touch a penny of it?' She asked the question knowing perfectly well that he had probably expected her to do just that. He had never been a mean man, but a million pounds was a lot of money, even to someone of Nick's enormous wealth. She could see it all. He had made the grand gesture, never thinking she would keep it. Actually her first thought had been to return his money, but Mr Farlow had refused to do so, insisting she wait a while and think it over. She was glad now that she had.

'No, I gave it to you in good faith. I thought at the time you deserved it,' he drawled, adding silkily, 'You were an exceptionally sensuous bed partner—so inventive.'

'Then you will be pleased to hear I spent it in a very inventive fashion.' She mocked his words, while stamping brutally on the memories he had evoked.

'You spent it all? I find that hard to believe, though I did wonder why Trevlyn needed so much outside backing when his fiancée is a wealthy woman.'

'Then let me put you mind at rest. I haven't a penny of your money left. Everything I own I have worked for myself. Your cash was spent in a couple of months.'

Abby was truly enjoying herself. It was an exhilarating feeling. Revenge was certainly sweet . . . Her green eyes glowed triumphantly into his guarded ones.

'And you can't wait to tell me how,' Nick prompted.

'I did have some help. Mr Farlow, my solicitor, arranged it all. The beneficiaries were the Battersea Orphanage, a retired actors' home, and—I just know you will appreciate this one, given your lifestyle—the Terrence Higgins Trust for AIDS sufferers.'

His mouth dropped open in stunned amazement as she spoke. Abby didn't hang around to see his reaction, but twisted out of his arms and made straight for the safety of the dining table, and the company of the others.

Michael greeted her with a wry grin and whispered, 'Dad's certainly enjoyed himself—a bit too much, by the look of him. Let's get out of here before he reaches the singing stage.'

Abby agreed. Nick had followed her off the floor, and she shot him a wary glance, expecting him to be furious. To her astonishment he was highly amused, his silver-grey eyes lit with laughter as he caught her look. Suddenly she felt exhausted. Why did she bother baiting him? She would never understand him in a million years, and she no longer had any interest in trying. Nick meant nothing to her now. He wasn't even worth her hatred.

Abby breathed deeply of the cool night air, relieved that they had finally made it to the steps of the hotel. The goodbyes had been protracted. Nick, in a complete about-face, had acted the sophisticated, charming host to perfection, so much so that Abby wondered if she had imagined his earlier anger. The five of them had been standing in the foyer of the hotel for the past ten minutes, while Nick had reaffirmed his intention of investing in the holiday complex, telling Harry he was returning to London in the morning and would instruct his legal department to get straight on with the documentation. Everything seemed sweetness and light, so why did Abby have this nagging sense of unease?

'Sorry about your fiancé,' a deep, mocking voice murmured in her ear.

Abby started in surprise; Nick was at her shoulder. She noted his disdainful glance at Harry and was immediately on her guard.

'Your lover won't be much good to you tonight, Abby dear,' he opined derisively.

'Nickie, darling, I'm cold; can we go up now?' The slightly slurred tones of Melanie's voice erupted on the cold night air.

Abby couldn't resist looking up at him with huge, innocent green eyes, shadowed with mock concern, she husked, 'My, Nickie, darling. You have changed—sunk to bedding drunks. How sad.'

'*Touché*,' Nick responded softly, and for a second she could have sworn it was pain she saw in his silver-grey eyes before he turned and walked back indoors.

Abby curled up in bed, hugging the flowered duvet around her slender frame. She said a silent prayer and goodnight to Jonathan, and, closing her eyes, looked for sleep, but the silence of her home seemed to taunt her. She felt completely and utterly alone, a bone-deep loneliness she had first experienced when her parents were killed in a plane crash.

They had been actors, her father with the RSC and her mother with a television series to her credit. Abby had known from an early age that she was a mistake which her parents did not quite know what to do with. A succession of out-of-work actors had been her nannies, until she'd been bundled off to boarding school at the age of eight. Her parents' only attempt at giving her a normal childhood had been the holidays in Cornwall. She had been fifteen when they died, and the shattering loneliness she had felt had caught her unawares. Mr Farlow, their solicitor, and Tony Bonajee, their agent, had been named as her trustee and guardian. Not that her parents had left much—an apartment in Kensington, and enough money to see her through school. For Abby, life had changed very little, except she had spent most of the holidays at school.

In retrospect, she could see what a shock it must have been for Tony Bonajee, a forty-year-old bachelor, to have a teenage girl to look after. He had tried his best, calling at the school and taking her out occasionally, and three days at Christmas on holiday in his flat in Mayfair. He had approved of her wanting to go to art school, and when, after only one term, she had realised she would never be another Turner, he had used his influence to get her a start in modelling.

Abby stirred restlessly, the thoughts crowding in on her. She had asked Tony to give her away when she married, and they had had their only argument. He wanted her to wait until he had made some enquiries about Nick Kardis. He knew the older Kardis, who had a very unsavoury reputation with young women. Like father, like son, he had said, but of course Abby had not listened.

If only she had . . . she could have saved herself an awful lot of pain. God, but she had been so naïve in those days. With bleak eyes, she lay staring into the darkness. She had built a good life for Jonathan and herself, and was content with it, but seeing Nick tonight had opened old wounds, stirred memories of her younger self which she had sworn to forget.

She had met Nick for the first time at the Ritz Hotel in London. It had been a huge society wedding. Anna, her only friend in the modelling world, had been marrying Eric, a career diplomat of independent means, and Abby had been their bridesmaid.

She had been standing on the steps of the Ritz, buffeted by the crowd waiting to wave the happy couple away, when a man's hand had closed over her shoulder in a steadying gesture. Anna's voice had rung out as clear as a bell.

'Watch that one Abby, darling. He's dangerous,' and, throwing her bridal bouquet straight at Abby, Anna had slid into the waiting Rolls.

Abby had blushed scarlet—and crushed the flowers in her hands, wishing she could sneak away to the room that had been reserved for her.

Abby turned over in the bed and angrily punched the pillow. Why hadn't she done just that? With hindsight, she realised that she had known deep down even then that she would never feel truly comfortable with the super-wealthy people, the sophisticated repartee that meant nothing. No, the pink marble of the Ritz was not for her, while to the Nick Kardises of this world it was a home from home. Unfortunately for Abby, she had ignored all the warning signs when a deep, amused voice had whispered in her ear, 'Will you marry me?'

Suddenly she had been aware of the warmth of the strong hand curving around her shoulder; she had turned, intending to freeze the man with a glance . . .

'No, thank you.' The words hung on the air, as the arresting quality of the man towering over her hit her like a punch in the stomach. His hair was night-black and curly, gently brushing the collar of the dark jacket that fitted his broad frame to perfection. His eyes sparkled silver-grey, a brilliant contrast to the tanned, ruggedly handsome face.

'Have I grown two heads?' he queried, his firm lips curving in a teasing smile.

'No, just one very attractive one,' she teased back, totally unlike her usual self, and all thoughts of leaving vanished.

'Allow me to introduce myself. I'm Nick Kardis, and you are?'

'Abby. Abby Jones.'

'Well, Abby Jones, you and I are going to dance the night away. I have been waiting for hours to get you on your own.'

'Have you?' She grinned up at him, completely bowled over by his charm. His arm slid around her shoulder, and his thigh brushed hers as he led her back inside. A delicious shiver coursed through her; no man had ever affected her so instantly before.

'Of course. Would I lie?' he mocked lightly, and, lacing his fingers through hers, he cradled her hand on his chest, his other arm encircling her waist. 'Now you are mine for the night, yes . . .?' and happily she agreed.

The rest of the evening took on a dreamlike quality. Nick swirled her around the dance-floor in his arms, and she felt as though she were floating on air. Between dances he told her he was Greek, with a home in Athens, but he was in London on business for his father who had recently had a heart attack and was not allowed to travel. He had attended the same public school as Eric's younger brother, hence his presence at the wedding and his near-perfect command of the English language.

For Abby it was magic. The blood bubbled in her veins, and she was wildly, gloriously happy. Nick made no attempt to disguise his admiration. His grey eyes sparkled into hers, and he dropped soft kisses on her glowing cheeks. He was obviously quite a bit older than her, but his ready smile was surprisingly boyish.

Finally the band played the last waltz and Nick pulled her gently into his arms and suggested it was time to leave. Holding her tightly to his side, he urged her across the elegant foyer to Reception. Abby could sense the tension in him, and naïvely thought it was because he was falling a little in love with her, and was nervous about asking to see her again, until he bent his dark head and, nuzzling her ear, whispered throatily, 'I think my suite will be best, sweetheart. It has a king-sized bed.'

The disappointment was so crushing that Abby couldn't speak. She acted on instinct alone, and, raising her hand, struck him firmly across the face with a resounding crack. She was oblivious to the amazed and amused faces of the other guests, and, storming out of the hotel, she jumped in a taxi and in seconds was on her way home.

What a fool! she berated herself. How could she have been so dumb? Obviously when he had asked her to spend the night with him he had meant it literally. He was the same as all the other men she had met in her short modelling career; completely immoral. But it did not help the ache in her heart.

The following day a huge bouquet of red roses arrived at her apartment. The card read, 'I'm sorry. Nick.' She snorted in disbelief, tore the card up, and gave the flowers to an elderly lady who lived in the flat above, determined to forget him.

The next day she returned late from an assignment. It was eight in the evening, and she was tired and hungry. Waiting on her doorstep was Nick Kardis . . .

Her memory had not done him justice, she thought helplessly. He was not handsome; he was lethal. He was dressed in a plain dark suit, a blue-and-white-striped shirt and silk tie. He looked every inch the successful businessman. His dark hair fell casually over his forehead, and his sensuous lips were curved in a wary smile of greeting. It was an effort for Abby to tear her gaze away from him, he looked so dynamic and very masculine, but she did, and, opening her bag, searched for her keys.

'What are you doing here?' she asked huskily, unable to deny the swift stab of pleasure his presence aroused in her.

'I want to apologise for the other night. I was out of line, I know. I thought because you were Anna's friend . . .'

Abby stiffened, and, clutching her key, attempted to fit it in the lock. She knew Anna was no virgin bride, but she resented his implication, though she could not really blame him. All men seemed to think models were there for the taking. It was an occupational hazard, and she was silly to feel hurt by it.

'I really am terribly sorry.' His long, tanned fingers curled about her wrist, his thumb carelessly caressing the soft underside, sending a shiver of awareness tingling up her arm. 'I did not mean to insult you. Only I wanted you so much, and I thought you felt the same. I rushed you and I'm sorry. My only excuse is that no woman has ever had such an instant effect on me before. I'm not usually so crass, I promise.'

Abby raised her head, her eyes locking with his. He looked genuine, and she wanted to believe him.

'Will you have dinner with me tonight? Please?' he asked softly.

'Yes, all right, and I—I—er——' she stammered. She could not argue with a contrite Nick, so finally she added, 'I'm sorry I slapped you, and if you don't mind calling back in half an hour I'll be ready.'

'No, I don't mind. I've waited here three hours, so another thirty minutes won't matter.'

She shot him a startled glance. 'Three hours?'

His grey eyes twinkled merrily. 'I could not take a chance on missing you, but it's all right, I'll just wait here like a lovesick swain, unless some kind person takes pity on me and offers me a drink.'

She chuckled, inordinately pleased that he had waited so long for her. 'All right. Come in.' And, opening the door, she ushered him inside.

Her apartment was the ground floor of a cleverly converted three-storey town house, and it had been her parents' pride and joy. She showed him into the lounge, and, crossing to the antique mahogany sideboard, carefully poured a large measure of whisky into a fine crystal glass. She did not drink much herself, but her father had always kept whisky in the house and she had unthinkingly continued the habit. She turned to hand him the glass and surprised an oddly derisive expression on his handsome face.

'This is a lovely room. You must be a very successful model,' he opined with a fine edge of cynicism.

It was her home, as familiar as an old shoe. Then Abby suddenly realised what he was getting at. Over the years, her parents had furnished it with style and elegance. A few excellent antiques were scattered around the room. A genuine Utrillo oil-painting had pride of place over the Adam fireplace. A large Chinese silk rug covered the centre of the room, framed by the highly polished stripped wood floor. She saw him eye the pipe-stand with an ironic smile. It was obvious he thought some man helped pay for the place. An imp of mischief made her refrain from telling him the truth.

'Oh, I don't live here on my own. Amy and a friend share the expenses, but they are touring on the Continent at the moment.' That sounded good, she thought gleefully, and no way was she going to tell this sophisticated man that the other two were penniless students, picking grapes in France. It would spoil her own sophisticated image.

In her room she showered and changed in record time, quickly slipping on a plain black sheath dress, cut low at the front to reveal the soft curve of her breasts, tiny shoestring straps over her shoulders the only support. She deftly applied her make-up, and, with a heart pounding with excitement, she picked up a black and gold lace shawl and draped it over her shoulders, chose a small clutch-bag and high-heeled black sandals, and she was ready.

His car was a low-slung racy sports model, upholstered in hide and smelling of leather and some tangy masculine fragrance that acted as an aphrodisiac on her spinning senses. Abby smiled up at him as he helped her into the passenger seat, her eyes following his lithe frame as he walked around the front and slid in beside her.

They drove out to a small restaurant on the banks of the Thames, where, seated at a secluded table in the corner of a dimly lit room, Abby thought she had died and gone to heaven. She was incapable of hiding the effect Nick had on her. They exchanged smiles, and he touched her hand in an intimate gesture.

'Allow me to order, hmm?'

'Yes, fine,' she murmured, his touch turning her to jelly. She forgot all about the disappointment of the other evening, completely enraptured by the raw masculine appeal of her companion.

The waiter appeared and Nick conversed briskly in French for a few moments, and the meal that followed was a gastronomic delight, but for Abby it might as well have been fish and chips. Nick occupied her every thought, his every look a caress.

'To us, and second chances,' he husked, raising his glass and gently touching hers.

'To us,' she whispered back, completely under his spell. She did not need the champagne to feel on top on the world; Nick's presence did that to her.

Over coffee he told her a little more about his business empire. He was an amusing and informative conversationalist, and she was soon completely relaxed and in no doubt that he took his work very seriously.

'I'm sorry, Abby. I must be boring you, but you're such a good listener.'

'No, you could never bore me,' she sighed. The deep velvet sound of his voice was a pleasure in itself. He could have been quoting the FT index and she would still have been enthralled.

His grey eyes gleamed with a mocking sensuous delight at her response. He knew what he was doing to her . . .

'Would you like to go on somewhere? Annabel's, or somewhere more intimate?'

If it got any more intimate, Abby thought helplessly, she would be crawling into bed with him. Something

she was not prepared to do. In that respect she was a very
old-fashioned girl. A vivid image of his naked body
gloriously entwined with her own made a blush rise up
her neck and shocked her back to reality. She hardly knew
the man . . .

'No, I have an early call in the morning for a mail-order
catalogue. I'd better get home.' She looked around the
room, avoiding the lazy, seductive smile curving his firm
mouth. She was surprised to note they were the only couple
left in the place, and it was after midnight.

The journey back to Kensington was completed in
silence. Abby was gripped by a fierce sexual tension she
did not know how to deal with. She was intensely aware of
Nick, the muscular thigh so close to her own, the long,
sensitive fingers curved lightly around the steering-wheel.
She felt an incredible urge to reach out and touch him, to
feel his hands on her flesh. She glanced at his handsome
profile, the generous curve of his lips, and wondered what
it would be like to be really kissed by him, not just the soft
exchanges of the other evening. He turned slightly, and
smiled at her with pure male appreciation of her femininity,
obviously aware of her intense regard and how it affected
her. Abby quickly looked away to stare sightlessly out of
the car window, embarrassed by her own wayward thoughts
and the ease with which he could read them.

The car stopped outside her apartment, and Nick deftly
unfastened her seatbelt, and then his own. Her heart
pounded like a drum in her breast, and she was convinced
he must hear it. She was incapable of moving. Would he
kiss her? Should she ask him in? Dared she ask him in . . .?
The decision was taken out of her hands as Nick leaned over
and, clasping her chin between thumb and forefinger,
tilted her face up to his.

'Ask me in for coffee, hmm?' Gently he lowered his
head, then his tongue licked softly around the outline of her
mouth, and it was the most erotic sensation she had ever
known.

'I'll make the coffee,' she sighed.

They had hardly made it into the lounge before Nick had

turned her swiftly into his arms.

'Forget the coffee,' he groaned. 'I've been aching to do this all night.' And his mouth found hers with devastating intent.

CHAPTER THREE

ABBY had been kissed before, and considered herself adept
at fighting off over-amorous males, but with Nick it never
occurred to her to resist. Her lace shawl fell unnoticed to
the floor as her hands clung to his broad shoulders. Her
mouth was warm and eager for his, and something
incredible fused between them as her lips parted to the
probing demand of his tongue. She closed her eyes and gave
herself up to the exquisite, hitherto unknown sensations
exploding within her.

In minutes they were lying on the long velvet sofa, and
Nick was pressing fervent little kisses on her slender throat.
A thousand nerve-endings tingled to life as his hand found
the round curve of her breast. His thumb, slipping beneath
the soft material of her dress, gently grazed one rosy nipple,
bringing it to instant rigidity. Abby moaned, and little
whimpering sounds of pleasure escaped her as, with
frightening expertise, Nick kissed and stroked her
trembling body. She could feel the rock-hard pressure of
his masculine arousal hard against her pelvis as he pinned
her to the sofa, his heavy thigh lying across her slender legs.

'You're beautiful, Abby; so very beautiful. Let me look
at you,' he growled, slipping the thin straps of her dress off
her shoulders. His silver eyes darkened to black as he stared
at her bared breasts. 'I want you, Abby,' he groaned. 'Let
me love you? I need to love you.'

Abby was mesmerised by the force of the desire in his
passion-glazed eyes. The word 'yes' trembled on her lips,
but never passed them, as the sound of a car backfiring on
the street outside sounded like a gunshot in the tense silence
and startled her back to reality. . .

Now, in the darkness of her bedroom, a slow smile
twitched Abby's full lips, then the smile broadened to a
grin, and the grin to a chuckle, until she was shaking with

laughter. The picture in her mind was so clear, she could see it as though everything had happened yesterday.

She had not laughed at the time. She'd been terrified, and, acting like the petrified virgin she had been, she had jumped off the sofa, and Nick . . . Nick had ended up on his butt on the floor, his jacket half off, his tie askew and, with his legs sprawled at right angles, his masculine arousal very evident. But the expression on his face . . .

Abby choked on her laughter. Even now, she could see him vividly in her mind's eye, incredulous, amazed, puzzled, hurt—no, woebegone, that was the word she was looking for. She had seen the exact same expression on Jonathan's face a hundred times, when she had taken his favourite toy from him and sent him to bed. With the back of her hand she wiped the tears of laughter from her eyes, and sighed.

Nick had not stayed hurt long, but had jumped to his feet, furiously angry, and had called her a vicious tease, along with a few Greek curses she could not understand, when she had told him to leave. Then, with a derisory glance around the elegant room, he had walked to the door and turned with a cynical smile on his lips.

'I should have known—you demand the trinkets, the diamonds first, but I'm not sure I want you that badly,' he had drawled mockingly, adding, 'I'll let you know!' as he slammed out of the flat.

Thinking about it now, from the comfort of her own bed, it slowly dawned on Abby that she had just taken a giant step forward. For the first time since her divorce she was able to look back and actually laugh at the great Nick Kardis. Perhaps finally she was mature enough to face up to her disastrous marriage and put it firmly behind her once and for all, instead of trying to pretend it had never happened. Yes, it was time to lay the ghosts . . .

She had not expected to see Nick again, after their disastrous dinner date, but in that she had been wrong . . . The following day she had walked out of the photo session, relieved it was over. She had scrubbed her face clean of make-up, and for once had not bothered about her appearance. Dressed in faded blue jeans and a sloppy sweater, the first things she had found that morning, she had decided to have a long walk, to blow away the cobwebs and her naïve dreams of love. Oblivious to passers-by, she set off at a brisk pace towards the nearest open space, the zoo.

'I'm sorry yet again.'

Abby's heart leapt in her breast at the sound of the deep masculine voice. She lifted her head, the memories of the previous evening bringing a blush to her cheeks.

'Nick.' She wanted to walk past him, but couldn't; her heart would not let her.

'Apologising to you is becoming a habit,' he said softly, taking her hand in his much larger one. 'You were right last night, I was being far too pushy. Dare I hope you will give me another chance? Third time lucky, hmm?'

For long moments she stared at him, the fast-becoming-familiar feelings exploding inside her. Somehow he looked younger, not quite so self-assured. He was dressed in casual hip-hugging jeans, and a soft lambswool sweater that clearly defined his muscular torso. She drank in the tangy male scent of his cologne along with every magnificent inch of him.

'Well, sweetheart? Will it be third time lucky?' he asked again, almost hesitantly, and her heart went out to him.

'I hope so,' she finally responded, a wide smile lighting her lovely face. 'But no more visiting my flat. How about the zoo?' she suggested, suddenly gloriously, wonderfully happy.

Nick laughed out loud. 'I hope that is not a dig at my animal-like behaviour of last night,' he teased. 'But if my girl wants to visit the zoo, so be it.'

It was perfect, a day out of time. They walked around the zoo hand in hand like two teenagers. Nick generously lifted a little boy, whose mother had her hands full with two more children, up on to his broad shoulders for a better view of the lions.

'That was nice of you,' Abby opined softly as they walked on.

'Not really, I like children. My sister has two and is

pregnant yet again. I spent a few days with them last month, and they wore me out.'

'I can't imagine anything wearing you out.'

'Oh, you'd be surprised. I was quite off colour when I returned to Athens.'

'You mean your tan faded,' Abby remarked cheekily.

'Watch it, girl, you look little more than a child yourself in that outfit. I may be tempted to spank you.'

'Ah, kinky, are you?' she joked, and ran as he made to grab her.

They ended up outside the monkey cages. The little animals were adorable until two started rather more serious antics. Ordinarily Abby would have laughed, but somehow with Nick beside her she was overcome with embarrassment, and flushed bright red. Nick chuckled and smiled down at her to share his amusement. Noting her flushed countenance, his intelligent eyes narrowed, then widened in surprise. Abby could almost see his brain ticking over, and tried to walk away, but he caught her by the arm.

'That's it. You are still a virgin!' he exclaimed.

'Will you shut up?' she groaned, looking desperately around. 'You don't have to broadcast it to the whole of London,' she muttered fiercely.

'I'm sorry. I should have guessed. Last night, that was why you chased me.'

Abby felt a complete fool, and meekly allowed Nick to lead her to a nearby seat, his arm a comforting weight around her shoulders. When she finally managed to meet his gaze she was stunned by the tender smile lighting his silver-grey eyes.

'Don't be embarrassed, Abby. You make me feel ashamed. Last night you were frightened, I see that now, and if I had not been so desperate to make love to you I would have realised what an innocent you are. My only excuse is that you always look so poised, so elegant, that it never occurred to me you were totally inexperienced. Today you look a bit like a child yourself, and it suddenly hit me. Just how old are you?' Nick demanded.

'I'm nineteen,' she told him, but did not add, only just.

'Fifteen years younger than me. Is that too much, Abby?'

'No, just perfect,' she sighed, her huge eyes telling him all he needed to know.

Three weeks later they were married in a civil ceremony at the local registrar's. Anna and Eric, back from their honeymoon, were the witnesses, and Tony Bonajee reluctantly gave Abby away. They flew to Paris for their honeymoon, and it was everything Abby had imagined and more . . .

Abby stared at the huge carved and draped four poster bed in the bridal suite, and was terrified. She knew it was ridiculous after a month of wanting, aching to be in Nick's bed, but she couldn't help it. She stood mute as Nick slowly began to undress her; the passion that had burned so brightly for weeks appeared to have vanished and she was overcome with shyness.

'Relax, my darling. It will be perfect, I promise. Trust me.' He whispered the words as his mouth explored her slender throat.

And she had . . .

With sweetly offered words of love and reassurance, he picked her up and laid her on the wide bed, his mouth covering hers in hot, drugging kisses that emptied her head, banishing her fears. He stepped back and shrugged off his clothes, then joined her on the bed. She gasped as he slid down beside her, his naked flesh burning into hers. Her blood quickened as his hands slowly caressed her, stroking up her ribcage, and flattening just below her breast. His long fingers teased and cajoled, while his lips covered hers, his tongue probing the moist, dark secrets of her mouth, inciting her response.

Abby's hands moved of their own volition to encircle his neck. She wondered how it would feel to touch him all over. Then there was no more time to wonder, as he moved over her to lie between her parted legs, his big body enveloping her. The rough hair of his chest rubbed against her swollen breasts until she whimpered with pleasure, her body electrified. He kissed her throat, her shoulders, his mouth hard and hot, and all the time his hands stroked down over her stomach, her thighs, every part of her.

His weight crushed her into the bed, his hips moving slowly, rocking against her. His mouth found the rigid tips of her breasts, suckling first one and then the other. She writhed wildly beneath him, her need of him shuddering through her, the emotion so intense that it was almost pain.

She felt one swift stab of real pain, then a delicious, hot, pulsating fullness as Nick thrust deeper and faster, possessing her completely. Her body screamed with tension, and she cried out as, with one final thrust, her body convulsed in a million explosive sensations, so intense she wanted to die with the ecstasy of it. Her heart stopped, then resumed its pounding. She felt the great shudders that racked Nick's huge frame, and she was flooded with a sense of oneness she had never known existed.

Nick rolled off her, and pulled her into his arms, his ragged breathing and the heavy drumming of his heart a testimony to his own fulfilment. The tears ran down her cheeks and mingled with the curling, damp hairs of his muscular chest. She was so full of emotion and the wonder of their love.

'I didn't hurt you?' Nick groaned.

'You could never hurt me, Nick. I love you,' she declared between sobs, her head buried on his chest, her slender body still trembling in the aftermath of their loving.

She had been wrong . . .

The first twelve months of their marriage were like a fairy-tale come true.

They travelled to every Troy hotel in the considerable chain, as Nick reorganised the leisure part of the family business. They returned to Greece and the family villa on Corfu for high days and holidays. It was a tradition in the Kardis family that they could not ignore. Nick's father insisted upon it. The older man had little to say to Abby, apart from asking her if she was pregnant yet. Nick's sister Catherine was not much more forthcoming. Her whole life revolved around her children and her husband.

In the summer, Abby and Nick settled permanently in

Athens, living in Nick's old apartment until their own home was built. Together they picked out a plot of land in the hills outside the city, and planned their house, intending to fill it with three or four children.

The only slight clouds in Abby's heaven were her inability to conceive, and Nick's father. His wife had died some years ago, and they quite often bumped into him when they were dining out in Athens. He always had a young woman on his arm, and never failed to ask Abby if she was pregnant. His behaviour she found disgusting, and she grew to hate meeting him.

Nick just laughed at her worries, explaining cynically, 'I respect my father as a businessman, and that's it. He has always had other woman. My mother knew about them and tried to ignore it; I do the same. Nothing will make him change—that's the way he is.'

'I still think it's dreadful,' Abby opined.

'Well, come on to bed and let's discuss it,' Nick drawled, and of course she did, but very little talking took place.

To Abby's surprise she discovered she was a very sensuous woman. Nick was an expert on eroticism and she his very willing pupil; they rarely spent a night without making love at least once or twice, and often more.

At Christmas he gave her the most magnificent diamond eternity ring, to match the huge diamond solitaire engagement ring he had insisted on buying for her. He was the most generous of husbands, and during their marriage had showered her with presents. An emerald necklace and bracelet, a gold Cartier watch, a ruby pendant—there was no end to his extravagance, and when she teased him about it he laughingly said, 'Who else can I buy jewellery for except my wife?'

Abby's present to him was a surprise Christmas cracker, and on Christmas morning, after a wonderful night of lovemaking, she knelt up on the bed and demanded he pull it with her. She watched with shining eyes as he opened the envelope that fell out and read the contents. Unbeknown to him, she had visited a gynaecologist, and it was a comprehensive report confirming there was nothing at all wrong with her and no reason why she should not have a dozen children. Excitedly she explained the temperature chart she was going to keep to be certain they made love at the optimum time for conception.

Nick grinned wickedly, pulling her down on top of him.

'My temperature is always high around you, sweetheart. All we need is practice,' he opined throatily.

They made long, passionate love, a feast of pleasure play that left them satiated in each other's arms. So it was all the more surprising to Abby when in the New Year things started to go wrong.

Nick began to work longer and longer hours; some evenings he arrived home so late that he slept in the spare bedroom. He explained that he did not like to disturb her, and she believed him. She trusted him completely. Gradually, as the weeks passed, her trust began to waver.

Abby tried to tell herself she was being silly, unduly suspicious, but Nick's behaviour when he was at home did nothing to allay her fears. He was as courteous and charming as ever, but somehow the spontaneity seemed to have vanished from their relationship, and, most telling of all, their sex life became virtually non existent. Oh, Nick still performed as well as ever, but Abby was shocked to realise it was always at her instigation, and 'performed' was the operative word. With a clinical precision he would take her to a shattering climax, then coldly turn his back on her and go to sleep.

Abby tried everything she could think of to hold his attention, convinced it must be her fault. She spent hours over her hair and make-up, she bought new clothes, and made herself look perfect for him, but nothing made any difference.

By the end of February she could not pretend to herself any more; something was desperately wrong, and one of the rare nights he was home and in their bed she tried to talk to him about it. Nick turned on her in fury.

'My God, woman, what do you think I am? A stud to perform on demand, when you've studied your bloody charts?'

Abby ran crying from the room, but there was worse to come . . . She tried to discuss their new house. It was almost finished. He told her bluntly to furnish it how she liked, he wasn't interested. It was too far out of the city, and he would only be there at weekends.

That weekend his name appeared in the gossip column of the local newspaper along with a photograph of him escorting an actress, Dolores Stakis, out of a city nightclub. Abby could not help herself; she asked him if he was having an affair with the woman. Nick laughed at her accusation.

'It's business, sweetheart. I'm backing her new film.'

'I don't believe you,' she cried. It hurt more than anything that had gone before to realise he could lie so easily.

'Please yourself, but a word of warning, Abby, dear. Don't become a clinging vine. I abhor that type of woman,' he drawled mockingly, and walked out of the room.

In the weeks that followed their marriage deteriorated into a hollow mockery. Abby, try as she might, could not ignore the rumours abounding around her husband, and at a party for the head office staff of Troy International, the night before they were to go to Corfu for the Easter, she was given concrete proof of his infidelity.

Nick danced once with Abby, then told her to mingle; like a dutiful wife, she did. A couple of hours later she walked out on to the balcony for a breath of air, and watched in horror as her husband slipped a gold bracelet on Melanie's wrist then, taking her in his arms, kissed her long and passionately. Abby wanted to scream as jealousy sharp as a stiletto pierced her heart. How she got to the powder-room she did not remember, but a few minutes later Melanie entered. Abby looked up at her with tear-filled eyes that widened with shock as the other woman spoke.

'Really, Abby, you should not let Nick upset you. I have known him for years, and he is never going to be a one-woman man, otherwise I would have married him myself. He is a great lover, though. So enjoy what you've got and be thankful,' she informed Abby with mock sympathy.

'Is that what you do?' Abby questioned sadly.

'Yes, why not? He is a very generous man.' Melanie laughed, deliberately eyeing the gold bracelet on her wrist. Abby didn't know how she controlled herself as Nick drove them home. He was at his sophisticated, urbane best.

'The evening went very well, I think. Don't you agree, my dear?'

She wanted to rant and rave at him, but instead murmured, 'Yes,' and remained silent until they got into the apartment. She turned on him as soon as he closed the door. 'Do you always give jewellery to your secretaries?' she demanded hardily.

His response struck her dumb. 'Oh, so you saw that. Well, there's no need to he childish, Abby. What's a small present or a kiss between friends?' he opined lightly, then added, his grey eyes narrowed angrily on her flushed, rebellious face, 'I've told you before, I don't like possessive women, and you are beginning to sound like one. I'm going to bed.'

Abby watched him walk into the spare bedroom, her eyes clouded with tears.

The following afternoon they arrived at the Kardis family villa on Corfu for the Easter break. In his father's house, Nick had to share a bedroom with her, and she watched him calmly walk naked from the shower and casually dress for dinner. Her eyes feasted on his lithe body, the golden tanned skin and rippling muscle. She wanted to scream aloud her frustration; it had been weeks since he had touched her, and even knowing he was unfaithful didn't stop her wanting him. Her body burned with suppressed longings, and the worst part about it was that Nick knew. Abby watched with infuriating helplessness as Nick walked out of the door, saying with a mocking gleam in his silver eyes. 'I will let you get dressed undisturbed. See you at dinner.'

Half an hour later, when Abby was seated facing Nick across the huge dinning table with all the family around it, Mr Kardis asked her the inevitable question. 'Not pregnant yet, girl?'

Abby raised her head and stared straight at her husband, all the months of pain and resentment bubbling up inside her. Her green eyes narrowed and became as hard as emeralds on his handsome face.

'It takes two, Mr Kardis, and your son is far too busy with other . . . things these days,' she drawled sarcastically.

There was a shocked silence—even Catherine's children were quiet—but Abby did not care. They could think what the hell they liked, she thought angrily, and, throwing down her napkin, she stood up and walked out of the room.

Nick caught up with her at the bedroom door, and she trembled at the fury in his steel-grey eyes. She heard the click as he locked the door behind him, and her heart leapt in her throat, but bravely she held his icy gaze, even as she backed away from him warily. Serves him right, she told herself. Why should she have to put up with his father's contempt while darling Nick remained whiter than white? In the next moment she would have given anything to take the words back.

'How dare you question my virility?' he demanded softly, the very lowness of his tone filling her with fear.

'I—I'm sorry,' she stammered, no longer feeling so brave. How could she have said such a thing in front of his family?

'Sorry? That doesn't begin to cover it, my loyal wife,' he drawled with biting cynicism, and, catching her by the shoulders, he drew her close.

'No. No, please!' she cried, the implacable determination in his steel-grey eyes telling her exactly what he intended. She shuddered as his fingers slid the long zip down at the back of her dress; then he slipped it off her shoulders so it fell softly to the floor. She wanted to scream at him not to take her in anger, but the words stopped in her throat as with slow deliberation Nick removed his clothes, carelessly throwing them over a nearby chair. An unholy excitement rushed through her at the sight of his splendid muscled frame, taut with a hint of ruthlessness. She was disgusted at her own reaction and blurted out, 'It will be rape, Nick.'

'Rape, never, but ravishment—oh, yes,' he said silkily, and, picking her up in his arms, he carried her across to the bed.

Abby drew a shuddering breath and gazed up at him, futilely searching his face for a sign of the love she had imagined they shared. He was smiling, but his eyes were flat and deadly.

'Don't look so frightened, Abby.' His finger trailed the outline of her mouth. 'I am not going to hurt you.' And, lowering his head, he closed his mouth gently over the pulse that beat madly in her throat. His hands swept lightly over her breasts and shaped her waist and thighs, as he bent lower and lower, his mouth grazing over her aroused nipples, her flat stomach.

To Abby's shame, her own traitorous flesh responded instantly to his touch. It had been so long that she could not disguise her need. She reached for his head, her hands plunging into the thick black curls, and she groaned out her delight as he lifted his head a fraction to suckle at her breast.

Then, shifting his body slightly, he slid his hands beneath her and lifted her to meet the hard thrust of his manhood. The blood coursed through her veins like quicksilver, and she was aware of the pulsing heat of him at the very centre of her being. He played her like a maestro, taking her to the brink again and again till every nerve in her body was screaming for release, and when the climax finally came it was shattering in its intensity. Nick collapsed on top of her, and for a while she was at peace, the ragged sound of Nick's breathing music to her ears. Then Nick rolled off her and stood up. She watched as he pulled his clothes on, waiting for him to say something, that he cared . . .

'If you want sex, you only have to ask. But don't ever again suggest in front of my family that I neglect my husbandly duties. Understand?' he demanded hardily, with no trace of emotion.

Abby understood all right. That was what she had become; a duty. She looked at him with pain-filled eyes, unable to say a word. For a moment she imagined she saw her own anguish reflected in Nick's eyes, but he turned and walked away, flinging over his shoulder, 'Pack your clothes. We are returning to Athens tomorrow.'

The end, when it came, was poetic in a way. Anna and Eric, at whose wedding the romance had started, also wrote finish on it. Out of the blue, Abby received an invitation to a reception at the British Embassy in Athens, and scribbled on the back was, 'Please come so I can catch up on all your news, Anna.' Eric had been appointed British Ambassador to Greece.

To Abby's delight, Nick agreed to attend, and on the day of the party Abby managed to shake off the apathy that had dogged her for months. Dressed in a new gown of green silk, and wearing the emeralds Nick had given her in happier times, she felt good, and more optimistic than she had done in weeks. Even when Nick called and told her to go on ahead as he was going to be a little late she wasn't too worried, but quite happily took a taxi to the Embassy.

Anna and Eric were delighted to see her, and accepted her apology for Nick's delay without question.Then, as the three of them stood talking, there was a stir at the entrance door.

'My God! Who invited that?' Anna exclaimed.

Abby turned to see what the commotion was about, and all the colour left her face. She wanted to scream. How could he do this to her? But instead she turned to Eric, the sympathy in his eyes almost her undoing.

'I'm sorry, Abby. I have no idea what that woman is doing here; she certainly wasn't invited.'

'The swine! I'll have them thrown out,' Anna insisted.

'Please, Anna, don't say anything.' Abby finally managed to speak. The guests causing all the mutterings were none other than Nick and, on his arm, the actress Dolores Stakis. The woman was dressed outrageously in gold harem trousers, her midriff bare and everything else only just hidden , and Nick was making no secret of the fact that he enjoyed the view.

Abby wanted to be sick, but her torture was only just beginning. With an arrogance only Nick possessed, he marched straight across to where they were standing.

Ignoring Abby completely, he spoke to Eric.

'Sorry I'm late, but I had to wait for Dolores to get dressed. When I told her I was coming here, she wanted to come along. I knew you wouldn't mind, old man,' he challenged.

'Did you?' Eric queried sardonically. 'Well, you were mistaken.' And, deliberately turning away, he slid his arms around Anna's and Abby's shoulders, saying, 'Come along, girls. There is an artist chap I want to introduce you to.'

'Eric, I love you,' Anna murmured. 'That was beautifully done.'

'Thank you,' Abby numbly agreed.

For the next hour Abby talked and danced with Ian Harkness, the artist, hardly aware of what she was doing. Until, with a rare sensitivity, Ian suggested she go home. Handing her into a taxi, he told her quietly, 'I'm breaking the habit of a lifetime, because I never give advice, but . . . You are much too young and lovely to waste your time on that man. Cut your losses and get out.'

Abby let herself into the apartment and looked around, finally admitting what she had refused to see for so long. The discreet lighting, the sunken-seating arrangement with the built-in music controls and dimmer switch. It was a bachelor's home, not hers, it never had been hers. She walked across to the sofa and sat down. She shivered—the temperature outside was touching ninety, but she felt numb, frozen. Surprisingly the door opened and Nick walked in.

She looked at him with a kind of emotional detachment she had not been capable of before. He was a handsome devil—women fell at his feet, and she had been no exception—but why had he chosen to marry her? On a whim, perhaps . . .

'Why, Nick? Why did you marry me? I thought you loved me.' She could not go on. She felt the seat depress as he sat down beside her, and, with a tenderness he had not displayed in months, he put his arm around her shoulders. Why now? she thought hopelessly.

'I married you because even I would not take a virgin as a mistress, and as for love—I love caviare, but as a steady diet it soon palls. You must see that, sweetheart.'

Abby had had her answer, and the tears began to flow. She cried until she could cry no more. Then Nick picked her up in his arms and carried her into the bedroom. Gently he laid her on the bed and, stripping off his clothes, joined her, gathering her into his arms as if she were the most precious thing in the world. He made love to her with all the passion and tenderness of when they were first married.

The next morning Abby awoke to find the bed empty, and pinned to the pillow that Nick's head had so recently occupied, a note. He was going away for three weeks to a month, cruising around the islands with Miss Dolores Stakis, supposedly looking for locations for her next film. Abby returned to London the next day. Ian Harkness had been on the same plane, and it was only his company that had stopped her breaking down on the journey.

Abby stared sightlessly into the night. Had she really been such a spineless creature? She had never seen Nick again from that night to this. Oh, she had waited in London, hoping he would come for her, and when she'd found out she was pregnant her first thought had been. Now Nick will love me again. Not even his rejection of her pregnancy in the lawyer's office had stopped her hoping. When Mr Farlow had sent her the degree nisi and copy of Nick's official disclaimer of the forthcoming child, only then had she accepted it was over. The agony and the grief had continued until she had held her son in her arms. She had looked at the tiny bundle of life and had been filled with an all consuming love for him, and an implacable hatred for the man who had denied her baby.

She flung the duvet back and, swinging her legs off the bed, got up. Pulling on her robe, she went into the kitchen and boiled the kettle to make herself a cup of instant coffee. Sitting down at the scrubbed pine table, she cradled the cup in her hands, taking an occasional sip as she reviewed the whole sorry mess. She cringed with shame at the naïve useless girl she had been at twenty. For years she had hated Nick, but now she could see it was a wasted emotion; the man wasn't worth hating. He was an attractive, virile male who enjoyed going to bed with women, but had little or no respect for them. The first couple of times she had met him, he had revealed his real character—or lack of it—but she had been too enslaved by his sexual magnetism to recognise it. It was her own fault. She had endowed him with all the characteristics she wanted in a husband, the chemistry between them having blinded her to the fact that he did not possess any of them. Once he had stopped taking her to bed every night, his true character had become plain. He would do anything to get what he wanted. He was as ruthless in his private life as he was in his business. He did not care what lies he told. She had no doubt that Nick told every woman he slept with that he loved them, and he did not see anything wrong in it. Look how he had agreed with Abby. Yes, he wanted a house, a family, anything to keep her thoroughly enslaved until he passed on to the next woman. That was what Abby had been; his sexual slave and nothing more. . .

She drained her cup and slowly walked out of the kitchen. She stopped outside Jonathan's room, and, pushing the door open, walked in. His toys lay scattered over the floor, and his first attempts at drawing adorned the walls. She sat down on the small bed, her hand gently stroking the Paddington Bear duvet.

Abby almost felt sorry for Nick Kardis. He was a shallow, immoral human being, and as such would never experience the true joys of life. Then, pulling back the duvet, she crawled into her son's bed. The slight baby scent of him lingered on the pillow, and she hugged it to her, then, with a soft sigh, fell into a peaceful sleep.

CHAPTER FOUR

THE gallery looked great. For the past hour Abby had cleaned, polished and dusted, and now, relaxing with a cup of coffee, she felt proud of her little domain and surprisingly content. She had got up this morning with a new lightness in her heart and a firm resolve to live life to the full. Her worst nightmare, meeting Nick again, had happened, and she had come through virtually unscathed.

She had dressed with care this morning in slim-fitting emerald-green trousers, and a multi-patterned green and black silk shirt. She had slung a broad black leather belt around her slender hips, with a saucy wink at her reflection in the long mirror. She looked good and felt even better. All her ghosts had been laid to rest, and over a hearty breakfast of ham and eggs she had found herself actually considering the possibility of resuming some kind of love life. For years she had kept her emotions, her sexual desire in cold storage, too afraid to do anything else—the emotional scars from her marriage had cut too deep—but now she felt strong enough to try again. There must be some decent men in the world . . .

Draining her coffee-cup, Abby told herself that it had been sheer bad luck that she had picked a bastard like Nick the first time. The next time she would be much more careful.

The door opened and Jonathan came tumbling in on the run, Iris a step behind him. 'Mummy! Mummy! Hello.'

Abby jumped up and, swooping down, swept Jonathan up in her arms, planting a smacker of a kiss on his little nose. 'I missed you, darling. Did you have a nice time with Aunty Iris? And were you a good boy?'

'Yes, Mummy.' He screamed delightedly as she swung him round, then gently lowered him to the floor.

'Can I go and play in the yard, please? I want to ride my bike.'

'Yes, go on, but be careful.' Abby pursed her lips in a kiss. 'Bye.' Jonathan was perpetual motion.

'I love you, Mummy.' He blew a kiss, and then the little figure was diving to the back of the gallery.

There was a playroom of sorts at the rear of the premises, that doubled as a store, leading out to a completely enclosed rear yard. It was a boon for Abby, because it meant Jonathan could quite safely play there while she worked.

'So, Abby, how did the meal go?' Iris asked, sinking into the chair Abby had just vacated. 'I swear that child has the energy of ten. I must be getting old; I don't remember my two ever being so boisterous.'

'That bad, huh?' Abby grinned. 'You're lucky—the dinner was verging on a disaster.'

'No . . . The deal hasn't fallen through, has it?'

'Don't worry, nothing like that, but . . .' For the next few minutes Abby described in detail the events of the previous evening, from the engagement, and the ex-husband, to Harry getting drunk.

When she had finished Iris asked quietly, 'Are you all right?'

Abby knew what she meant. It was Iris who had watched her pick up the pieces after Nick. 'Oddly enough, I've never felt better. The marriage was a mistake, I can see it quite unemotionally now, and it could never happen again. The silly young girl who made it doesn't exist any more—thank God! In fact, I found myself thinking that being engaged to Harry is not a bad idea. He would make a good father for Jonathan.'

'No!' Iris exclaimed forcibly. 'He's far too old for you.'

Abby looked in amazement at the telling flush on her friends face. Iris and Harry, of course! Why had she never realised? She could kick herself for being so insensitive to Iris's feelings. 'I was only joking,' she reassured her friend, and added, changing the subject, 'Why not have the rest of the day off? You deserve it, after a night with Jonathan.'

Iris took no persuading, and after she had left Abby thought of going to check on Jonathan, her full lips curved in a smile.

'Hello again, Abby.'

Unconsciously her spine stiffened at the sound of that deep, velvet voice. Oh, no, she groaned inwardly. Nick Kardis.

'I thought you would be halfway back to London by now,' she said bluntly. She might have laid some ghosts last night, but if they were going to keep appearing in the flesh they were liable to become very irritating. And what flesh, Abby thought detachedly. Nick was leaning against the door frame, his long body clad in a black lambswool sweater and hip-hugging jeans. With his dark good looks, he appeared like a panther, lithe and lean, and he certainly had the instincts of one. What was he here for? she wondered uneasily.

'I am going back today, but I could not leave without seeing your place of business. You sounded so proud of it last night that you aroused my curiosity.' Straightening up, he wandered nonchalantly around the room, stopping here and there to look at a particular picture, then moving on.

Abby crossed to the desk and sat down. She wished she hadn't two seconds later, when Nick casually sauntered over and perched himself on the corner of the desk. His muscular thigh, outlined beneath the taut fabric of his jeans, was only inches from where her hands lay on the desk. She had the strangest urge to reach out and touch him. Oh, no, she told herself, and hastily clasped her hands in her lap. Her emotions may have come to life again, but not for Nick Kardis, of that she was certain.

She eyed him warily, sure it was not only curiosity that had brought him here. 'Do you see anything you would like, sir?' she asked facetiously to mask her unease.

'Yes, I do, but I'm not sure I can afford your price,' he drawled mockingly, subjecting her to a slow, leisurely scrutiny that made her want to slap his smug face. 'The landscape by Ian Harkness is excellent. I gather he is a personal friend of yours. I saw his painting of you on the beach at an exhibition in London last month. It's very good, though I prefer you in the flesh, myself,' he opined suggestively, his grey eyes lingering on the V neckline of her shirt.

Abby clenched her hands in her lap, her brain flashing

warning signals that she did not want to acknowledge. It was a coincidence that Nick was in St Ives. Nothing more. She had to believe that; the alternative was too disquieting. It had been a coincidence that she had met Ian Harkness again. They did happen. Two years ago he had come here for the summer and he had bumped into Abby on the beach. He had done some sketches of her, and when she'd refused to pose for him he had asked if she minded his painting her from the sketches, She had agreed, because by then he had already held his first exhibition in her gallery, so helping her business enormously. Now she wished she hadn't. Nick's voice broke into her thoughts, and she looked up at him, her wary eyes trying to assess just what he was up to.

'Tell me, did Harkness help you finance this place, or was it your fiancé? Someone must have done if you were telling the truth last night.'

Abby breathed a sigh of relief—perhaps it was only the money that was niggling him. 'I didn't need any financial help. I sold my apartment in Kensington, and London property prices are so inflated that it allowed me to buy this place with plenty to spare.' She could not keep the pride out of her tone. She knew Nick had thought of her as a helpless nobody, and it was very satisfying to tell him how wrong he was.

'The apartment was yours? I thought you rented it with two other girls.'

'No, I shared it with Amy and Tim—students, in fact. I promised them they could stay until they had finished college, and as it happened it worked out very well. I returned to London the same summer they completed their courses. They have an advertising agency in Manchester now,' she informed him smoothly.

'So you are a truly independent lady,' he mused, and, sliding off the desk, he moved around to stand towering over her.

'Yes, and I intend to stay that way,' she informed him, fighting down the fear she could feel curling in her stomach at his proximity.

'Trevlyn agrees, does he?' he asked softly.

Abby's gaze had slid to his wide shoulders tapering

down to lean hips, and for a second she lost the thread of the conversation. 'What?' She snapped back to attention.

'Trevlyn, your fiancé,' he mocked.

She had forgotten all about the bogus engagement, but suddenly saw it as a godsend. 'Harry is a wonderful man, and fully appreciates my desire to have a fulfilling career.'

'I'm not surprised. He is far too old to fulfil your other desires,' he drawled suggestively.

Abby had to fight to stop the colour flooding her face, and, furious with herself for letting him rile her, she determined to put an end to the conversation. 'Well, if there is nothing you want to buy,' she picked up a pen, 'I do have rather a lot of work to do, so . . .'She tailed off.

She felt rather than saw him bend over her. She kept her eyes firmly fixed on the papers in front of her, but his fingers caught her chin, their pressure hard as he forced it up until he could look into her face. She recoiled at the anger icing his grey eyes.

'You are not really going to marry Trevlyn?' The words came out harsh and clipped.

'I don't think it is any of your business,' she responded, puzzled at his odd behaviour. If it wasn't the money that angered him, what else could it be?

'And supposing I make it my business? I wonder how Trevlyn would react if I told him you like more than one man at a time,' he threatened insultingly.

Abby shoved his hand away and leapt off the seat. She was sick of his veiled insinuations, of both last night and today, and she did not have to put up with them. 'Not everyone has your morals—or should I say lack of them?—and I would be obliged if you would leave.' She made to walk past him, but Nick caught her arm, his long fingers biting into her tender flesh, effectively restraining her.

'Take your hands off me.'

'Not until I'm ready,' he snarled.

Abby faced him, refusing to back down at the tight-lipped fury evident in his hard face. She did not know what was niggling him, and she was not interested in finding out. She just wanted him back out of her life. 'Look, Nick, let's try and behave like two civilised adults. It was nice seeing you again, and goodbye.'

To her surprise it worked. Nick dropped her arm and walked away. He stood in front of a small seascape, apparently studying it, but she could see the stiffness, the tension in his large frame, as if he was struggling to control some emotion.

Slowly he turned, his eyes clashing with hers, then sliding to focus somewhere over her shoulder.

'You're right, of course. What you do is none of my concern. I apologise for the remarks I made.'

An apology! She could not believe it . . .

'Actually, I came—I came——' stranger and stranger, a hesitant Nick '—I want to see the boy.'

Abby never knew what her response would have been, for at that moment Jonathan came running in.

'Mummy, Mummy, I broke my truck.' His bottom lip trembled as he valiantly tried to hold back the tears.

She dropped to her haunches, all thought of Nick forgotten as she tried to console her son. 'It's all right, darling,' she said, and, taking the truck from his small hands, she deftly replaced the wheel and tyre. The same thing had happened before, and she had intended taking it back to the toy shop, but somehow had never got around to it. 'There you are, my pet, as good as new.' Straightening up, she smiled tenderly down at him.

'Thanks, Mummy. You're clever.' With a sniff and a wave, Jonathan darted back outside. She watched his retreating figure; he was a sturdy little boy and the joy of her life.

'Trevlyn was right . . . with those looks there is no mistaking he is a Kardis.'

Abby stiffened and turned back to Nick. She caught a glimpse of shocked horror on his handsome face, and her mouth twisted into a disdainful grimace. She guessed what he was thinking. He was so obvious that it was disgusting. There was no denying Jonathan's parentage, and when the boy grew up he might go to Nick demanding involvement in the family firm as his due. Nick's Greek sense of family honour would not allow him to refuse, but in fact that would not suit him at all; he had never made any secret of the fact that he was determined to control the mighty Kardis business empire entirely on his own. When they were married he had often argued with his father, because the old man insisted on retaining a controlling interest in the company even though he no longer did any work.

'Jonathan may look like a Kardis, but, thank God, only on the outside. His character is uniquely his own. There is not a devious bone in his body. He is totally honest, both emotionally and morally, and I intend to make sure he stays that way,' she informed him bluntly, and for a second, as her green eyes clashed with grey, she imagined she saw pain in their silvery depths. She almost laughed out loud at her own foolishness. His look was as cold and remote as the Arctic Ocean. Cynically she continued, 'You have nothing to worry about, Nick. *My* son,' she emphasised the possessive pronoun, 'will never make any demands on you.' It was as if she had never spoken.

The ring of the telephone prevented him from replying, and she was grateful. Oddly enough, Jonathan had not yet asked about his father, and she lived in dread of when he would, because she had no idea what she was going to tell him. Ignoring Nick, she crossed to the desk and picked up the receiver.

'The Hope, Abby speaking.' She listened for a second.

'Hold on a moment, Harry,' she said, lowering her voice huskily, and, placing a hand over the receiver, she glanced up at Nick.

'I am rather busy, and we have nothing more to say to each other, so, if you don't mind . . .'And with a toss of her head she indicated the entrance door. To her surprise and relief, he made no comment, but turned on his heel and walked away. Abby grimaced as he stopped, the door half open. Now what?

'Just one question, Abby. Does Jonathan know who his father is?'

Her mouth fell open in amazement. 'His father?' she

exclaimed scornfully. 'You've got to be joking!'

'A straight yes or no is all I require,' he demanded.

'No. You disowned him four years ago; he doesn't have a father.'

Nick closed his eyes and swayed against the door; for a moment she thought he was going to faint. His huge frame shuddered, and his wide shoulders slumped as though the weight of the world had fallen on him. Abby took a step towards him, then checked herself. What had happened? Was he ill? she wondered. Their eyes met, and she recognised a look of such torment in the deep silver depths that she was struck dumb. She hesitated, not knowing whether to offer help or ignore his obvious distress.

'Goodbye,' she mumbled, and, taking her hand off the mouthpiece of the telephone, she deliberately lowered her voice. 'Sorry, Harry darling, a customer.' She was a fool to be worried about Nick Kardis; he was more than capable of looking after himself. She heard the door close and breathed a sigh of relief. Nick had gone, hopefully for good, she thought, only half listening to Harry. Her ex-husband affected her more than she wanted to admit.

Harry's abject apology for drinking too much the night before finally concluded, and Abby had to stifle a laugh when he told her that he had called Antonio and Maria to inform them the engagement was all a hoax.

'What's so funny?' he asked gruffly. 'I thought you would be pleased.'

'Oh, I am, Harry, I am.' She was amused by her earlier idea of maybe marrying Harry. A sober Harry was obviously petrified at the thought she might have taken him seriously, and with her good humour restored she replaced the telephone.

The rest of the day passed uneventfully.

For the next few days, Abby jumped every time she heard the door chimes. Her common sense told her she was being stupid, there was no reason for Nick to come back, but the seed of doubt, planted in her mind when Nick had told her he had seen the painting of her, would not go away. Was Nick's reappearance after all these years an honest coincidence? She wasn't sure.

It was Harry who convinced her in the end. A fortnight later he informed her jubilantly that all the documents for the project were signed and it was full speed ahead for the holiday complex. Nick's agent in London was in complete control, and there was no likelihood of Mr Kardis's returning, except perhaps for the official opening in a year or so. By October, Abby had banished him from her mind.

'Can we go now?' Michael asked in exasperation.

'Yes, but don't you forget, the first sign of a cloud in the sky and you come straight back,' Abby ordered. 'Have you got the waterproofs? And don't forget the hamper.'

'Abby, for heaven's sake, we are only going around to the next bay. The boat is built like a tank with sails added—hardly your laser racing yacht. The boy has his lifejacket on, and we aren't even out of the house yet. What more do you want?'

Abby chuckled. 'Yes, you're right. Go on with you.' Bending down, she gave Jonathan a big hug and pushed him out of the door. She watched until the two figures disappeared from sight, grimacing at her own overprotectiveness. Jonathan was going to have his first taste of sailing, and she was worried sick. Telling herself Michael was a fine, responsible adult didn't help much. She knew she would be on edge until they returned, and with a heavy step she walked back upstairs to the living-room.

The church bells were ringing out loudly on the early morning air, calling the faithful to the eight o'clock service. Abby wandered into her bedroom and eyed her unmade bed with disgust. It was no good, she knew she would not be able to go back to sleep, although she'd had a late night last night.

The previous evening she had gone out to dinner with Ian Harkness. Her lips twitched with amusement; she could still see in her mind's eye the look of stunned amazement on his face when she had accepted his invitation. He had called yesterday afternoon to discuss his forthcoming exhibition, and out of habit had asked her out, knowing she always refused. When she had happily accepted he had pretended to faint.

Abby shrugged off her housecoat and pulled on her raggiest pair of jeans and a disreputable, paint-stained sweatshirt. Actually she had surprised herself last night. She had thoroughly enjoyed the evening. Ian was a witty and amusing companion, and when he had walked her to her own doorstep, and taken her into his arms, she had discovered he was also a very experienced lover. The kisses they had shared had aroused a pleasant tingling sensation in Abby, but had been in no way threatening. She had not asked him into her home as Michael and his girlfriend had been baby-sitting, but they had parted with a promise to see each other again on Monday.

Yes, Abby told herself, busily straightening the duvet over the bed. She was a whole woman again, able to enjoy a man's embrace without fear. It was ironic that she had the meeting last month with Nick Kardis to thank for it. The ringing of the telephone interrupted her train of thought, and, sitting down on the bed, she picked up the extension phone.

'Abby here.'

'Could I speak to Nick?'

Abby shook her head. Was she hearing things? His name had just been in her thoughts.

'I said, can I speak to Nick? Can you hear me?' It was Melanie, but why on earth was she ringing here?

'Yes, I can hear you, but what's going on?' Abby finally found her voice.

'Surely Nick spent the night with you?' Melanie's high-pitched laugh trilled over the wire. 'You're not making him wait until you are married again, Abby? You're hardly a virgin, darling.'

'I'm sorry to sound so obtuse, but I haven't the slightest idea of what you are talking about. I have not seen Nick——' And before she could add that she had no desire to. Melanie interrupted, all sweet concern.

'But he should have arrived in Cornwall yesterday. He called me from Exeter to check on his father. He was supposed to arrange the reconciliation with you over dinner last night. I do hope he hasn't had an accident.'

'Reconciliation? What reconciliation?' Abby spluttered. Was the woman mad?

'I knew you'd be thrilled. I told Nick so.'

'Thrilled?' She was horrified.

What followed left Abby pale and trembling with rage. She wanted to smash something, preferably over Nick's head. Melanie was most forthcoming. Nick's father had had a dodgy heart for years, but after his latest attack the doctor had told Nick the old man would not last another six months. Nick, devious, devilish Nick, had to produce a grandchild in double-quick time or see his father's shares in the company go to his sister's children—something he was not prepared to let happen. His solution was quite simple—a quick remarriage to Abby, with her ready-made son, and Nick would get what he wanted, as always . . .

Abby slammed the phone down, too angry to be polite. She jumped off the bed, her lovely features contorted with fury. She stormed into the living-room. 'Damn Nick! Damn him to hell,' she muttered under her breath, her thoughts so bitter that she could taste them. She had no doubt that Melanie had spoken the truth. It was just the kind of arrogant, arbitrary plan Nick would dream up. Well, he was in for a rude awakening, Abby vowed.

How could she have been so dumb as to believe Nick's reappearance in her life had been pure coincidence? But she had. What a blind fool she had been. Distractedly she ran a slender hand through her tumbled mass of hair, sweeping it off her brow; she needed to think . . . What was she going to do when he turned up? Slam the door in his face? No, he would keep on trying.

The ringing of the gallery chimes echoed through the empty building. It could only be Nick—all her friends used the rear entrance when the place was closed for business. Reluctantly, Abby walked down the stairs into the deserted gallery, hesitating before opening the door. She would listen to him calmly and then throw him out. It might be interesting at that, she told herself. She wouldn't mind betting every penny she possessed that he would not tell her the truth. The doorbell rang again and she hurried to open it.

'Why, Nick!' she exclaimed, with exaggerated surprise, and for a second she nearly did slam the door in his face. His dark eyes slid down the length of her body with a possessive arrogance that made her blush. He appeared more dynamic than she remembered from their last meeting. He exuded a raw animal magnetism which his softly tailored suede jacket and hip-hugging chinos seemed designed to enhance. Before, she had thought he looked his age, but now, with the early morning sunlight slanting across his rugged features, his black hair tussled by the breeze, there was a sense of power, an inherent vitality about him, that reminded her forcibly of the Nick she had met and married! A *frisson* of fear slivered down her spine. Perhaps it would be wiser not to let him into her home.

'Abby, may I come in?'

'I'm closed today.' But she was talking to his back, as he brushed past her and ascended the stairs two at a time. Shutting the door, she ran after him. 'Now, wait a minute.' she spluttered, finally catching up with him, standing in her living-room, looking as if he were lord of all he surveyed. 'You can't barge into my apartment like this.'

'Where is the boy?' he demanded, his gaze sweeping the room and coming to rest on Abby.

'Jonathan is out sailing,' she informed him with deceptive calm, while underneath she was burning with resentment at his high-handed attitude.

'Is that wise? He is only three—rather young to be out sailing,' Nick opined sharply, his face turning pale beneath his tan.

How dare he question her actions? she fumed, her green eyes darkening with temper. 'It is none of your concern what my son does, and in the circumstances, you are the last person who should be offering advice.'

The corner of his mouth twisted in a wry smile. 'I suppose I can't blame you for thinking that way, but I am his father. It is only natural that I should worry about him.'

Abby swallowed with difficulty the crude expletive that had leapt in her throat, and in an effort to control her baser instinct, which was to crown him with the nearest large object she could lay her hands on, she crossed to the sofa and sat down. Proud of her self-control, she informed him smoothly, 'I was not aware that you were anybody's father, and certainly not my son's.'

'It is no good denying it, Abby,' he declared softly, his gaze lingering on her pale face.

Was it tenderness she saw in his dark eyes? Impossible . . .

'After I left here the last time, I did some checking—something I should have done years ago. I am Jonathan's father. There can be no doubt about it.'

'My God! You're incredible,' Abby blurted, incensed at his presumption. 'I seem to remember you officially disowned my child long before he was born. You? A father? You've got to be joking! You don't even know the meaning of the word.'

'Have you finished?' Nick asked quietly, subjecting her to a slow, intent appraisal that left her feeling as if she had been assessed and found wanting.

Suddenly Abby was very aware of her tattered jeans and paint-splattered T-shirt, and some inner voice told her to stop arguing and get rid of him as quickly as possible. His anger she could face, but this quieter Nick posed a much bigger threat. 'Yes. Yes, I've finished.' They had been finished years ago, and there was no benefit in raking over the ashes. 'Just tell me what you came for, and go,' she commanded.

'Can I sit down?'

'Why so polite? You barged into my home without asking,' she reminded him sarcastically.

He made no comment, but moved with lithe, long-legged grace to sit down on the sofa beside her, and before she could protest he had caught her hands in his. Abby tugged to free herself—the warm clasp of his large hands and his nearness made her edgy—but his fingers tightened their grip just enough to hold her captive.

'Please, Abby. I want to talk to you, to try and explain.'

'Try' being the operative word, Abby thought waspishly. With Melanie's information fresh in her mind, her curiosity was aroused. It might be fun to string him along, just to hear what kind of intriguing explanation he would come out with. Schooling her features into what she hoped was an expression of pleasant anticipation, and forcing herself to meet his gaze, she prompted encouragingly, 'Explain what, Nick?' She had succeeded. There was a swift flash of what looked suspiciously like triumph in his silver-grey eyes, quickly masked.

'Oh, Abby, you make me feel so ashamed. On my way here this morning I was convinced I would have to bludgeon you into listening to me. I should have known better. You were always prepared to give me another chance in the past, and you haven't changed,' he said softly, and, sitting forward on the sofa, he held her hands loosely against his warm thigh.

Abby parted her lips over pearly white teeth in what she prayed was a sweet smile, and demurely lowered her thick lashes to hide the fury in her eyes. The ego of the man was truly stupendous; he would try any trick in the book to get his own way. His fingers were gently stroking her hand, and it took a massive effort in self-control not to tear away from him.

'I know I treated you abominably in the past, and I don't expect you to forgive me completely, but in time I hope to make you forget. When I divorced you I truly believed it was for the best that we parted. I freely admit I was a fool. I made a disastrous mistake and, God knows, I've suffered for it over the past few years, but now I know the truth and I want to make it up to you and our son.'

A mistake, he called it. He had almost destroyed her, and he had the colossal nerve, the audacity, to sit here and calmly tell her it had been a mistake ... It took every ounce of will-power she possessed to remain seated. She drew a deep, calming breath. 'Make it up? Make what up?' she queried silkily.

'I want to marry you again. To put the past behind us. To make a proper home for our son, become a real family,' he declared hardily.

Abby's head shot up and she glared with barely concealed amazement into his handsome face. He was smiling . . . Actually smiling! She wanted to scream. How dared he blithely assume he could walk back into her life and lay claim to it? She had been prepared for his proposal, Melanie's words emblazoned on her mind, but for Nick to bluntly come out with it like that was still a shock. Her lips moved, but she could not get the words out, too furious to make sound.

Nick, seeing her struggle, put completely the wrong interpretation on her silence. He dropped her hands and enfolded her in his arms, his mouth closing over hers in a long kiss. Numbly she lay in his arms as his lips trailed along her cheek, his breath warm on her ear, before she recovered her senses and realised what he was up to. She pushed him away and leapt to her feet, almost running across the room.

She clasped the window-ledge, her knuckles white with the strain, and, breathing deeply, she fought down the trembling in her stomach. The familiar view of the bay, the sea shimmering gold in the morning sunlight, gradually calmed her quivering nerves.

A mistake. We will marry again. A kiss. And that was it . . . He had not even bothered to think up a plausible story. Why was she surprised? she asked herself bitterly. He had treated her as a brainless fool before, and he obviously thought she still was. The conceit of the man was enormous—one kiss and the little woman safely enslaved again. Well, he was in for a rude awakening . . .

Nick came up behind her; she could feel the warmth of his body reaching out to her. Determination stiffened her spine and slowly she turned around, lifting a hand to stop him coming any closer. 'No,' she said. Just one word . . .

'Abby, please hear me out,' he pleaded, his long arms hanging loosely by his sides. He made no attempt to touch her. 'I didn't mean to grab you like that, but I lost control.

It's been so long since I held you, kissed you, I couldn't resist the temptation.'

'You never could,' Abby injected bitterly. That was his trouble, he could never resist the temptation with any woman.

'I know what you're thinking, Abby, but you're wrong, and if you will just give me the chance I'll prove it to you. I need you, and Jonathan, and I swear I will do everything in my power to make you happy. You've got to believe me, Abby. I promise I won't pressure you into a sexual relationship until you're ready.' His grey eyes, dark with emotion, bored into hers, as if they would possess her soul.

For a moment she was almost taken in by the sensual warmth, the pleading in his silvery eyes, then she remembered exactly why he needed her . . . Her jaw tightened and she stared angrily at him; he had almost fooled her again. 'No . . . I don't believe a word you say,' she declared coldly.

'You don't believe me,' Nick murmured. His fists clenched, and the colour drained from his face, leaving him white and oddly tense. 'Why does that surprise me?' He asked the question of himself, and turned away from her. His broad shoulders slumped, he strode the length of the room.

Abby watched, as he rubbed his hand around the back of his neck to ease the tension, or more likely to give himself time to think up another story, she thought cynically.

'Damn it, Abby!' Nick swore, and spun round to face her. 'I didn't want to admit the truth, but if it's the only way, I'll do it,' he said tersely.

Abby relaxed slightly. This hard-faced man was the Nick she had seen so often in the past, his true self. . .

'Remember the Christmas you gave me your gynaecologist's report saying you were fine? Well . . .when we returned to Athens, I also went to see the doctor, but I was not as lucky as you. He told me I was sterile.' He turned and paced up and down the room, avoiding looking at her.

Abby's mouth dropped open in amazement; it couldn't be true. Her eyes skated over the long length of him. He was in peak condition, sleek-muscled, with tight buttocks, blatantly masculine—a more virile man would be impossible to find. Still, she had to give him full marks for inventiveness.

'You can't imagine what it did to me, Abby. I was angry, shattered, almost suicidal. Your only interests were the home we were planning and the children we would have, and I knew it was a waste of time. I realised I had to let you go. You were young enough to marry again, and you deserved a man who could give you children. At first I was going to tell you the truth, but I couldn't be that selfish. I knew you loved me and would never willingly leave me.'

Abby's lips tightened in an angry line; she hated to be reminded of how besotted she had been with him.

'So I had to destroy your love. I had to make you leave of your own free will.'

'How very noble of you,' she couldn't resist inserting.

Nick stopped pacing only a foot away from her, and shot her a quizzical look. Coldly she outfaced him. She didn't believe a word, didn't want to . . .

'Noble I thought I was at the time, now I know I was a fool. I should have double-checked, but I guess at the time I went a little crazy. So now you know why I behaved the way I did. I hurt you badly, but I hurt myself more . . .'

Abby had to count to ten before she dared speak. So he'd known she'd loved him, and would never have left him. That might have been true once, but never again, she vowed, and as for his hurting—nothing short of a knife through the heart would ever hurt Nick Kardis. She allowed none of her anger to show as she responded with dry cynicism. 'You mean, you forced yourself to take a mistress or two and it was all for my benefit? How very unselfish of you. And divorcing me for desertion——' that still rankled—it was Nick who had gone off on a cruise with Dolores, and yet he had had the bare-faced cheek to cite Abby's desertion as grounds for divorce '—how kind,' she drawled mockingly, and watched with some satisfaction as the flush spread up his handsome face. At least he had the grace to blush.

'Put like that, it does seem improbable, I know, but it is the truth. The affair with Dolores was all an act—she is an old friend of mine and she agreed to help me out.'

'Now that I do believe—the "old friends" bit. Poor Melanie has been hanging around for years as well, and God knows how many more.' Abby no longer bothered to disguise her disgust. What kind of fool did he take her for? Only an idiot would believe him. Wearily she wondered why she felt disappointed. His lies in the past had been equally transparent. She wished he would just go and leave her alone; she could feel the onset of a headache . . .

'Abby, I swear I was never unfaithful to you.' To lend credence to his words, he grasped her by the shoulders, his thumbs pressed up under her chin, forcing her face up to his. His silver-grey eyes burned down into hers, sapping her will to resist, and for a long moment they stood motionless. Abby's heart lurched in her breast, the pulse in her throat beat an erratic tattoo beneath his palm, and she was transported back in time, the want and desire flaring in his eyes a potent reminder of all they had once shared.

Her body, with a will of its own, swayed towards his hard strength as though recognising its master. Helplessly she stared at him. Her mind told her he was worthless, but her body had suddenly reawakened in a shameful response to his potent masculinity. Why now? she groaned inwardly, and fought to control her racing pulse. Then Nick spoke, and his words snapped her back to reality with a vengeance.

'I have never made love to another woman since the day I met you. Four long years I've ached for you, Abby.'

His dark head bent towards her, but swiftly she wriggled out of his hold. The stunned expression on his handsome face was probably the first genuine emotion he had shown since arriving, she told herself bitterly. 'You should have stopped when you were ahead, Nick. You almost had me there.' Her tone was scathing, mainly because she was furiously angry with herself as well as him.

'What do you mean?' he demanded hardily.

'Overkill, *Nickie darling*. Four years? Really? You couldn't go four days without a woman,' she scorned. His grey eyes narrowed angrily, and he took a step forward, but she deftly moved to one side, and before he could comment she added, 'Why don't you try telling the truth for a change? At least then I might have some respect for you. As it is, I think you are beneath contempt.'

'I have told you the truth,' he said softly. 'I'll swear it on a stack of Bibles if you like,' he offered, still quietly, but with an underlying edge of steel.

For a second Abby wondered if she was making a terrible mistake, then she quickly banished the thought. She had told Nick herself that she was pregnant, and Jonathan was the living proof that his story was all lies. No. Her mistake had been letting him in her home in the first place . . .

'Don't bother, Nick. I wouldn't believe a word you said if you slashed your wrists and wrote it in blood, and now I think you'd better leave,' she concluded coldly.

'You bitch!' he snarled. 'You don't give a damn, do you?'

'I should have thought that was obvious, even to someone with your over inflated ego,' she retorted bitingly. 'Did you really think you could walk back into my life, just when it suited you, and spin some sad story, and have me fall at your feet in gratitude? Well, buster, I have news for you. I wouldn't marry you again if you were the last man on earth, and as for getting your hands on my son—you can forget it.' She tried to pull her arm free, but his hand was like a vice as he dragged her hard against him.

'You really do hate me,' Nick grated, his gaze intent upon her flushed and angry face.

'You'd better believe it!' she snapped, trying once again to break free. Surprisingly, he let her go . . .

Abby rubbed her injured arm, warily watching Nick's retreating figure. Thank God, he was leaving. But he didn't . . . His hand on the half-opened living-room door, he turned back, his eyes hardened until they resembled polished steel, and Abby felt the first tendril of deep fear stir in her stomach.

'I want my son, Abby, and I always get what I want.'

The implacable determination in his tone warned her that he had stopped playing games. 'You and I are going to be married next week. If you are in any doubt, I suggest you have a word with your fiancé Trevlyn.'

'Harry? I don't understand,' Abby faltered, badly shaken.

'It's simple enough, my dear. Trevlyn has put every penny he has or could borrow into the leisure centre, on the assumption it will be completed in a year.'

'But all the documents are signed. You can't drop out.'

'I don't have to. My legal department inserted a clause in the small print. We don't need to complete it for five years. I reckon it will take about eighteen months for Trevlyn to go bankrupt, but of course his workers will be redundant long before that. It's a shame about the village—quite a pretty place, I thought—but these things happen,' he drawled mockingly.

Abby's brain spun with the implications his threat portrayed.

'You wouldn't do that?' she queried thickly, her mouth dry with fear.

Nick's lips twisted in a satanic smile. 'Try me, Abby.'

'You're despicable!' she cried.

'Perhaps, but I want you and Jonathan, and I don't care what I have to do to get you. I will be back this evening for your answer, and in the meantime I suggest you have a word with Trevlyn. He will confirm the facts, and then the decision is yours . . .'

CHAPTER FIVE

ABBY stood trembling with frustrated rage, unable to speak as Nick walked out with a wicked grin, slamming the door behind him.

She had no illusions left where Nick was concerned. She didn't trust a word he said. His puny excuse for his past behaviour she dismissed as a casual, arrogant attempt to obtain her willing co-operation. My God! she thought bitterly. He'd certainly changed his tune fast enough when he'd realised she wasn't swallowing his story. His last remark about the Trevlyn contract she unfortunately could not dismiss so easily; a sinking sensation in the pit of her stomach warned her that Nick at the end might have been telling the truth. She recalled his triumphant, cynical smile as he'd left. It had been Nick at his unscrupulous best . . .

Her first thought was to tell him to go to hell, Trevlyn Cove was not her responsibility, but it was quickly followed by the realisation that she could not do that to her friends, and Nick, the swine, knew it. His coming back into her life was no accident, and she, poor fool, had convinced herself it was coincidence.

Abby sighed, her anger draining away like air out of a burst balloon, and collapsed into the nearest armchair. There was nothing she could do until Nick's story was confirmed, and she could not see herself asking Harry outright about his business deals. But perhaps Michael—yes, of course, he could tell her what she needed to know. After all, it was Michael, at twenty-five and a qualified architect, who had come up with the idea for a holiday complex on the headland at Trevlyn Cove in the first place.

He had designed the luxury package incorporating both indoor and outdoor facilities, two swimming-pools, a gym, jacuzzi, tennis-courts, even an eighteen-hole golf course, and, at his brother David's instigation, a cable car to the foot of the cliff, and a diving school. There were plenty of wrecks around the bay, from the square-rigged *Neptune* lost in 1869 to the steamer, *The Bessemer City*, lost in 1936 and anyway, diving was the love of David's life. She knew that finding finance had been difficult, as Harry had insisted on investing every penny he could scrape up for a seat on the board and overall control of the workforce, the idea being that his soon-to-be-redundant miners would be employed before anyone else, but out of the blue a multi-national company had contacted him and all his problems had been solved. Unfortunately for Abby, it looked as if hers were just beginning.

Jonathan burst into the room, his little face flushed rosy red with the sea air, chattering excitedly about his day out. 'We went all around Trevlyn Cove, and the men are digging at the bottom of the cliff. Michael says they are making a huge lift before the weather gets bad.'

With a few judicious questions to Michael on Abby's part about the possibility of delay, her worst fears were confirmed.

'Don't mention delay to Dad. He has borrowed heavily to buy as many shares as possible, on the assumption that once the place is operational his salary as chairman and managing director will pay the high interest on his loans. Any more than six months' delay and we'll all be in Queer Street.'

'That's just great,' Abby opined, the irony in her tone earning her a sideways glance from Michael.

'Is something bothering you, Abby?' he asked quietly.

'No, no, of course not.' She smiled. 'Sit down and have some tea.' It would do no good telling Michael her problem. This was something she was going to have to work our for herself. How? She had no idea . . .

Later Abby stood naked in the shower, the needle-sharp spray doing nothing for her quivering nerves. A few tears mingled with the warm droplets of water slithering down her cheeks, as the enormity of her problem finally sunk into her tired mind. Jonathan was fast asleep, worn out from his day on the boat and innocently unaware of the turmoil his natural father was about to cause in his young life.

Abby racked her brains trying to think of some way out. The idea of a custody battle for her son filled her with horror, but it would be preferable to marrying Nick Kardis again. She cursed long and fluently under her breath. Nick was smart. A court case would take months and he might not win; also, according to Melanie, Nick's father did not have many months left. No. Nick needed to get Jonathan as quickly as possible, and that meant remarriage.

Abby groaned in self-disgust as she remembered her mature, rational conclusion of a few weeks ago that Nick was not worth hating. She must have been soft in the head. Hate was too tame a word for how she felt about him. She despised him with every fibre of her being. Four years of contentment, even happiness, destroyed in one morning. There was no way she could stand spending the rest of her life with Nick. It would be a living hell . . .

She turned off the shower and, picking up a large, fluffy pink towel, wrapped it sarong-style around her body and walked out of the bathroom. She came to an abrupt stop in the middle of the bedroom floor, as the solution hit her. The helpless, almost defeated expression faded from her green eyes to be replaced with a tentative glimmer of hope.

Of course . . . It was obvious. She did not have to spend the rest of her life with Nick; when his father died she would be free . . . Suddenly things did not look quite so bad. Nick had never wanted her or Jonathan, he wanted them now purely for business reasons, and once his father was gone he would not give a damn what Abby did. She breathed deeply, a new determination stiffening her spine. It would be hard, but she could do it. The effect on Jonathan of spending a few months in Greece should not be too bad—he was young, and once they returned to their life in St Ives he would soon forget.

It was a different Abby altogether who opened the door half an hour later to her ex-husband. Gone was the paint-splattered girl of the morning, and in her place was an elegant, mature woman. She had dressed with care in a straight camel-coloured wool shirt with a matching Viyella checked shirt; and she hoped she looked businesslike.

'Hello, Nick.' She barely spared him a glance before turning on her heel and heading back upstairs, with a curt, 'Close the door behind you.' She did not stop until she reached the living-room, and then she swung round, her chin tilted at a defiant angle, and faced him.

'Such a pleasant welcome, Abby darling, and hello to you too.'

His grey eyes captured hers, and he was laughing at her. She felt a startling upsurge of anger and wanted to knock the smile off his handsome face, but, like a magician producing a rabbit out of a hat, he presented her with a huge bunch of red-gold chrysanthemums.

'Flowers for my lady,' he declared in a throaty drawl.

She flinched, he had done it deliberately, she knew. Before they were married he had often brought her flowers, and used the same words; she had replied with a curtsy and, 'Thank you, kind sir.' But not any more, never again, she vowed.

'Thank you, I'll put them in water,' she responded stonily, and shot out of the room into the kitchen. She swore violently as she opened a cupboard and took out a vase, then filled it with water, sticking the blooms in like a bunch of celery. She sensed Nick had followed her, and quickly she blurted into speech. 'I'm surprised you found a florist's open on a Sunday.'

'I didn't. I was driving around and saw a greenhouse full of flowers—they reminded me of the colour of your hair, so I persuaded the owner to sell me them.'

Abby's lips twisted in a cynical grin. She should have guessed, Nick always got what he wanted, from a huge company to a simple flower. 'You shouldn't have bothered,' she told him bluntly. As she turned, her hand shook slightly as she placed the vase on the table. Nick was much too close for comfort. Her businesslike appearance belied her quivering nerves.

'So gracious, Abby. You surprise me,' he mocked, and, lifting his hand, he caught a loose tendril of her hair.

'I was right—they are the same colour.'

Abby swallowed a lump that had inexplicably formed in her throat, and, stepping back, she sped around the table, putting some space between them. Her green eyes sparked angrily.

'Sit down and I'll make coffee,' she instructed tightly switching on the already prepared percolator. She wasn't about to put up with his flirtatious ways, and the sooner he realised it, the better.

'Here in the kitchen?' Nick asked blandly.

'Yes. I think we can dispense with the pleasantries and get on with our business. You can pretend this is a boardroom table,' she told him facetiously, carefully filling two cups with coffee.

'Business?' One dark brow arched mockingly. 'Most ladies of my acquaintance would not equate a marriage proposal with business,' he opined drily.

'Humph!' she snorted inelegantly, placing the cups on the table. 'They obviously don't know you as well as I do.' And, pulling out a chair, she sat down, breathing a sigh of relief as Nick took the chair opposite and followed suit.

'I can't argue with you there, Abby. No one knows me as intimately as you do.' His large hand covered hers where it lay on the table, and for a moment she was mesmerised by the darkening gleam in his grey eyes. 'I have vivid memories of how you delighted in discovering every centimetre, every single pore of my skin,' his deep-throated voice drawled seductively.

Erotic images of their naked bodies entwined filled Abby's mind for a second, and it took all the will-power she possessed to pull her hand away. Grasping her coffee-cup with both hands, she took a great gulp of the hot liquid.

She ignored his blatantly sensuous comments, and, with studied calm, replaced her cup on the table and plunged straight into her carefully prepared speech.

'I despise blackmailers, but in this instance I have no choice but to agree to your proposal, as you are perfectly well aware. There is no way I could let you destroy the prosperity of my friends. But I want you to understand that I know the real reason for this marriage, and once . . .' Abby hesitated. She had been about to say, once your father is dead, but it sounded too callous, so she substituted it with, 'Once you have got what you want, that is it . . . we are free to live our own lives. Agreed?' She did not see the startled, wary look Nick shot her, and when she raised her eyes to his, demandingly repeating, 'Agreed?' his usual mocking smile was firmly in place.

'Certainly agreed,' Nick responded with alacrity. 'I'm glad we understand each other, Abby. I'll finalise the wedding arrangements and we'll be married on Saturday. In the meantime I want to get to know my son, and explain things to him.'

She stiffened at his mention of Jonathan. 'He's asleep now, and any explanations necessary will come from me.' Her reply was curt. She knew her feelings weren't logical, but it was one thing to think you were being used and quite another to have it confirmed so speedily. A dent to her feminine pride, she thought ruefully. Nick's voice broke into her thoughts.

'As you wish, but I want Jonathan told I am his father.'

'No!' The exclamation escaped her, then, forcing a calmness she did not feel, she added, 'I don't think that's very wise.' She did not expect to be with Nick for long, and she saw no reason to upset Jonathan—he was too young to understand the machinations between adults.

'Yes, Abby, I insist.' Nick's hard, intent gaze held hers and she was the first to look away.

Perhaps he was right, she thought resignedly. After all, he had agreed to their parting again in a few months, hadn't he? She could afford to be generous. Some day Jonathan would have to be told who his father was; maybe it was better now, when he was still young enough to forget again.

'All right,' she agreed quietly, and, pushing her chair back, stood up. 'I think that covers everything, so if you don't mind I would like an early night. It has been a trying day,' she concluded drily, and walked purposely towards the door, intending to show him out, but she never made it, as Nick moved like greased lightning and blocked her exit.

'Not quite everything,' he opined, his hand curving around her jaw, forcing her to face him.

'What else is there? The time and place I have no doubt you will let me know later, so . . .' Her voice was cool, but it was taking a terrific effort of will to maintain the polite façade. She stood perfectly still, only inches away from him, the intensity of his narrowed gaze, his height and breadth, intimating in the small room.

'Aren't you forgetting the little matter of your fiancé, Trevlyn?' Nick queried silkily.

He was right, she had forgotten. Hastily she lowered her lashes, disguising her expression from him as she answered, 'Harry and I broke our engagement a couple of weeks ago. We decided we were better suited as friends . . .'

'Than lovers,' Nick prompted cynically.

Abby did not correct him. Let him think what he liked. God knew she had had to live with the knowledge of Nick's other lovers for long enough before.

'That is none of your business, Nick. Harry and I are just good friends. That's all you need to know.'

'True, but I'm curious. I know you have a great sexual appetite, and you're a very beautiful woman—there must have been a string of *admirers* in the last few years.' He spoke softly, but the fingers holding her chin tightened until she could hardly breathe. She searched frantically for a flippant response, but the glittering menace in his steel-grey eyes knocked every thought from her mind except the desire to escape. 'Harkness for starters. Get rid of him.'

His dark gaze raked her body and she shivered as though he had touched her, at the same time she puzzled over how he knew about Ian. She had gone out with the man for the first time last night, and, more to the point, why was Nick acting as if he cared? She opened her mouth to ask, but before she could say a word his arms closed around her like bands of iron, hauling her hard against his taut, muscular frame while his mouth covered hers, his tongue thrusting, plundering her inner sweetness in a kiss of powerful, savage possession.

Abby tried to pull free, but to her horror her own body betrayed her, as a storm of feelings she had thought long dead surged through her like a tidal wave, breaking down all her defences. He had caught her completely off guard, and when he broke the kiss and stepped back she was left reeling with shock; the force of the emotions his kiss had aroused horrified her.

Nick cupped her face with both hands, saying, 'Don't worry, Abby, you won't be frustrated—the addiction is still there.' She wanted to slap the triumphant, mocking smile off his face, but, reading her intent, he dropped his hands and stepped smartly back. 'I have business in London tomorrow. I'll be back on Tuesday, and don't forget—get rid of them. I don't share . . .'

She stared at him, her quick anger vanished. 'What?' she asked, stunned by his comment. Surely he did not expect her to share his bed . . .?

'You heard, Abby. When you are back in my bed, it will be only me you think of, I can assure you of that.'

'But you can't mean to sleep——?'

'Sleep is not what I have in mind,' he taunted ruthlessly.

'B-but,' she stammered, 'I thought . . .' What had she thought? A renewal of their physical relationship had never once occurred to her . . .

'Thought what, Abby? That you and I could live together platonically?' A cynical smile curved his sensuous mouth and his grey eyes looked mockingly down at her. 'What was it you said this morning? I couldn't go four days without a woman.. . You were always a match for me in that department, *dear*. So what does that tell you?' he queried silkily.

Abby was incapable of stringing a sentence together, her heart still racing from the effect of his embrace.

'Nothing to say, Abby?'

'B-b-but . . .' Wide-eyed, she stared at him, her thoughts in chaos. His lips parted over white, even teeth in a grin of genuine amusement, as he delighted in her confusion.

'Odd, I don't remember your having a speech impediment before.' He chuckled and with casual arrogance lifted her chin with one long finger. 'Don't look so surprised, Abby, darling. We will have a full and normal marriage, and judging by your reaction to my kiss you will thoroughly enjoy every second of it. Now get that early night you wanted—you look as if you could use it.' And, trailing his finger up to her lips, he added softly but with deadly intent, 'Remember, I don't share.'

Long after he had left, Abby was still leaning against the door-jamb; she did not trust her legs to carry her one step. She knew Nick meant what he had said. He was not the type of man to deny himself the pleasures of the flesh, and if Abby was the only one available he would quite happily use her. She groaned out loud at her own incredible stupidity. Her early conclusion that a few months in Greece would not be too bad now seemed hopelessly naïve. Obviously Nick was without a lady-friend at the minute. Of course, there was always Melanie, she told herself. But one woman had never been enough for him, as she knew only too well.

Wearily she straightened up and walked along to her bedroom. She slowly stripped off her clothes and crawled into bed. The events of the day, the emotional upheaval, had left her too exhausted to think straight, and thankfully she closed her eyes and fell into a deep, unconscious sleep.

She was up early, the faint light of dawn barely entering her room as she struggled out of bed and into the bathroom. She was pale-faced and heavy-eyed, her body still exhausted although she had slept like the dead. Abby could not believe the events of the previous evening. She had been so confident, and Nick had agreed so readily to her demand for freedom when the time came. She felt like a general who had won the battle but lost the war. Nick's parting shot that theirs would be a normal marriage for the time it took had absolutely floored her. The touch of his lips on hers had almost sent her into shock, and her stomach clenched in pain at the thought of what his complete possession would do to her.

Like a robot, she woke Jonathan, washed and dressed him, gave him his breakfast, and they set off for playschool. She barely heard his ceaseless chatter. It was only when she felt a sharp tug on her hand and his little voice raised indignantly—'Mummy, you've walked straight past Ben's house and he has to come with us!'—that the fog in her mind lifted.

She looked down and saw the worried frown on Jonathan's face and a wave of anger shook her—at herself for neglecting her priorities. Jonathan and her friends, the life she had made for herself meant everything to her. Standing in the middle of the pavement, she looked around the peaceful little harbour and made a silent vow to herself that she would do whatever she had to to make sure that by next summer they were back here in this beautiful town, living as they did now.

She spent the rest of the day grappling with the problem

of how to tell everyone of the approaching nuptials and sound convincing. She managed to drop casually to Iris that Nick Kardis had called the day before, testing the water, so to speak, expecting cries of outrage. Instead, to her amazement Iris remarked prosaically, 'Well, it is only natural the man would want to see his son. As he's Greek, I can't understand why he has not done so before. They are notoriously fond of their children.'

Abby almost snorted indignantly, but stopped herself in time. Once she had believed that sweeping generalisation, until she had told her husband she was pregnant, and been quickly disillusioned.

Later that night, lingering over coffee at The Cove Country House, she rehearsed in her head ways of telling Ian she was leaving for a few months. Since their rather passionate parting on Saturday night, it was obvious he thought they had progressed from good friends to something more, and it was with regret that she opened her mouth to explain, but that was as far as she got. Her eyes widened in horror as over Ian's shoulder they clashed with cold, calculating grey ones. Nick strode across the restaurant with casual arrogance and, before she was aware of what he intended, planted a hard kiss on her open mouth.

Then, straightening up, he placed a proprietorial hand on her shoulder, and turned a deceptively bland face to her companion.

'Harkness, isn't it? Thanks for looking after Abby for me, but you must let me pay for the meal. I'm so sorry I did not get here in time to join you,' he drawled in an insolent apology.

'What the hell do you mean barging in here, Kardis? Abby is no longer yours,' Ian declared coldly, while Abby was too stunned to say a word. How dared Nick imply she had been expecting him? He wasn't supposed to come back until tomorrow.

'Abby darling,' Nick's fingers bit into her shoulder as he favoured her with a blatantly sensuous look, 'surely you have told your . . . friend . . . we are getting married again?'

'My God! Are you crazy, Abby?' Ian exclaimed. 'The man nearly destroyed you before. You can't possibly go back to him.'

'She already has. We spent last night together,' Nick stated flatly, all pretence of good humour gone. 'Didn't we, Abby?' he demanded, his grey eyes glittering down into hers, daring her to defy him.

She was furious. One look at Ian's crushed expression and she wanted to tell him the truth. He was a true friend and did not deserve to be so humiliated, but even as the words of denial formed on her lips she knew she could not utter them. Nick's fingers were like talons in the flesh of her shoulder; she could feel the leashed tension in his taut frame, and, much as she would have enjoyed proving him a liar, she did not dare do it. With an infinitesimal, fatalistic shrug of acceptance, she gave into Nick's domination.

'Yes, it's true. I am marrying Nick again.'

'You're a fool, Abby!' Ian jumped up from the table, ready to storm off, then hesitated—perhaps it was something in her expression—and, turning to Nick, he snarled, 'I don't know how you've managed it, Kardis, but I intend to find out.' Then, with a bitter-sweet smile for Abby, he added, 'Remember, if you ever need a friend. I'm always available for you.' Then, throwing a handful of notes on the table, he walked out.

'How touching,' Nick sneered.

Abby was too choked to speak, and made no demur when Nick grabbed her arm and ushered her through the restaurant and outside to his waiting hire car, a dark blue Mercedes.

She could feel the rage slowly building up inside her as Nick expertly manoeuvred the big car through the dark country lanes to St Ives. On arriving at the gallery, Abby unfastened her seatbelt and jumped out of the car, her front door key ready in her hand. She had no intention of allowing Nick inside, but he was too fast for her, and as she would have closed the door in his face he pushed his way in. She turned her back on him without a word and marched upstairs.

Michael, once again acting as baby-sitter, could not hide his surprise when she rushed into the living-room, Nick only a step behind her.

'My, my, Abby, that's fast work. You go out with one man and come back with another,' he joked.

Abby had to force herself to smile; when really she felt like screaming blue murder. Nick, on the other hand, with an audacity that left Abby goggle-eyed, had Michael convinced in five minutes flat that their divorce had been a mistake and their remarriage was a certainty. Michael left with a knowing male smirk for Nick and a tender smile for Abby.

'I'm glad for you, Abby. Nick is a fine man and Jonathan needs his father.'

She waited until she heard the front door close, then turned on Nick, almost spitting nails. 'How could you? How dare you?' she stormed. 'All those lies trip so easily off your tongue, first to Ian and now Michael. Regret . . . Love . . . Mistake . . . Baloney, more like. My God! You're incredible.' Her voice rose an octave as she spoke, and she was physically shaking with suppressed rage, but before she could give full rein to her temper Nick caught her by the shoulders.

'Shh. Abby, you don't want to wake my son.'

She had forgotten about Jonathan, and immediately lowered her voice, hissing angrily, 'He is *my* son and——'

Nick cut her off sharply. 'He is *our* son, and I gather from that last crack that you haven't told him yet that he has a father. I warned you last night, Abby, if you didn't tell him, I would. You've had twenty-four hours to explain it to him. I've already wasted four years; I'm not going to lose another day.'

The sheer, unmitigated gall of the man took her breath away. She shrugged his hands off her shoulders and stepped back, putting some space between them. Her green eyes flashed brilliantly with contemptuous anger. *'You? You* wasted four years? That's a very convenient memory you have there—as I recall, it took you all of two seconds to disown my baby and me——'

'Abby, I bitterly regret what I said that day, but there were reasons.' He interrupted her in full spate, his hand reaching out to her, but she slapped it down.

'Yes, Dolores Stakis and the rest,' she sneered. Too angry to recognise the flash of pain in his dark eyes, she carried on, 'Hmmph! Now you need the boy, you expect me to what?' One perfectly shaped brow arched derisively. 'Get him up in the middle of the night and say, "By the way, this is your father.

Sorry he wasn't around before, but your grandfather's dying and you have to meet him so your daddy can get the biggest share of Troy International."Jonathan will love that,' she jeered mockingly.

'What did you say?' Nick bit out.

'Oh, come on, Nick. Why carry on the pretence with me? We both know the truth. You admitted it last night when you agreed so quickly to let Jonathan and me go when the old man dies,' she told him bluntly.

Nick's mouth tightened. 'Who told you about my father?'

Abby willed herself to calm down—she was exhausted, and her last remark had been tactless to say the least, but what the hell? A bit of honesty between them might make the next few months more bearable. 'Melanie told me.'

'When did you speak to her?' Nick demanded, his eyes narrowed intently upon her flushed face.

'She rang me yesterday morning, before you arrived.'

He frowned at her answer. 'I see,' he murmured, almost to himself, then, turning, strolled across to the sofa and sat down.

Abby watched him warily. His strong brown hands were clasped together between his knees, his dark head bent forward. Had he been anyone else she would have thought he looked utterly dejected, but not Nick Kardis. More acting? she wondered. Slowly he raised his head, his full lips twisted in a wry smile.

'Well, I knew you had a low opinion of me, Abby, with some justification, but so low——'

'The pits,' she confirmed curtly.

She caught a flash of anger in his grey eyes before he closed them for a second. When he next looked at her his expression was bland, no trace of any emotion visible.

'You look tired, dear, and I certainly am. I think we might as well call it a night and get some sleep,' he opined softly.

'Certainly, let me show you out,' she responded, relieved he was finally going. She turned towards the door.

'There's no need. I have not got a room booked at the hotel until tomorrow. I'm staying here the night.'

Abby stopped in the doorway and swung round to face him. 'Here?' She drew a shaky breath, and unconsciously straightened her shoulders. 'No way.' It should have sounded adamant; unfortunately it came out more like a squeak.

His mouth twitched. 'Don't look so worried. I'm not going to share your bed. At the minute I feel more like strangling you than making love. So go and get me a couple of blankets, there's a good girl.'

For a moment she hesitated, toying with the idea of throwing him out. Her gaze slid from his broad shoulders to his long legs. No, it was a physical impossibility. Turning on her heel, she marched out.

She returned a couple of minutes later, the blankets in her arms, and stopped dead just inside the lounge door. Nick had removed his shoes, jacket and tie, and was busily unbuttoning his shirt. She flushed, recalling how he had always slept naked, and, throwing the blankets in the general direction of the sofa, she beat a hasty retreat, grinding her teeth as his mocking, 'Goodnight, Abby darling,' followed her along the corridor.

It took her ages to get to sleep; the thought of Nick lying on the sofa in the next room did nothing to help.

Abby groaned as tiny fingers plucked at her eyelids.

'Mummy, Mummy, wake up. There is a strange man in the living-room. A huge man.'

Groggily she looked up into the small, cherubic face of her son. His big eyes were wide and fearful.

'That's all right, darling,' she muttered, still half asleep. 'It's just——'

'Your daddy,' a deep voice intoned.

Abby sat up in bed, clasping the sheet to her breast, the forceful masculine tone an alien sound in her bedroom. Her green eyes widened with horror as the import of the words registered in her sleep-hazed mind. How could he be so tactless? Nick, a smile of rare tenderness illuminating his handsome face, was standing in the doorway, his gaze intent upon the small boy sitting on the bed.

'M-m-my daddy?' Jonathan stammered. 'I thought you were dead.'

Oh, no, I can't face this, Abby thought helplessly, and closed her eyes. It was worse than she had ever imagined.

'Is that what your mummy told you?'

The voice was closer now, and, as the mattress depressed, she slowly opened her eyes. Nick was sitting on the bed next to Jonathan, but his steel-grey eyes, icy with contempt, locked on to hers. Abby flinched as though he had struck her, and, breaking the contact, she turned to stare down at her son, a mixture of guilt and puzzlement reflected in her expressive features. She could understand Nick's anger—obviously he thought she had told Jonathan his daddy was dead. She hadn't . . . She had no idea how his little mind had come to that conclusion.

'No one told me.' Jonathan's little voice broke the growing silence, and, moving closer to Abby, while never taking his eyes off the strange man, he added, 'I guessed.'

'What a funny thing to guess,' she prompted, trying to smile and ease the tension that seemed to surround the three of them. Her stomach churned sickeningly with fear for her son. She would never forgive Nick if his blunt statement of fatherhood hurt Jonathan in any way. She put a protective arm around his small shoulders.

'Not really, Mummy,' he chirped, much more confident now he was safely ensconced in his mother's arms. 'I asked Aunty Iris, and her daddy's dead, and I asked Uncle Harry and his daddy's dead, and I asked Uncle Ian and his daddy's dead, and you told me your daddy's dead.' he stopped in amazement. 'And my friend Ben's daddy's dead, he told me so, so there . . .' Ben's lack of a father was obviously the clinching argument in his young mind. 'So I thought my daddy was dead, see?'

Abby chuckled at his indisputable logic. He really was an amazing child, she thought, and she hugged him briefly to her side. 'Well, darling, you thought wrong because——' Before she could finish the sentence, yet another voice intruded.

'Abby, Jonathan—come on, lazy-bones. You've slept in—it's nearly nine.'

'Iris . . . 'Oh, hell!' Abby swore softly under her breath as the older woman burst into the bedroom and stopped dead, her mouth hanging open at the sight of the apparently cosy trio.

Jonathan jumped off the bed and shot across to Iris,

stumbling over the words in his haste to tell her the news.

'Aunty Iris, th-that . . . that man says he is my daddy.' He raised one arm, a chubby hand waving excitedly in the general direction of Nick. 'And he stayed here *all night*.'

The last words were said with such drawling emphasis that Abby was vividly reminded of just how much like his father he was. She shuddered to think what Iris was imagining, but one look at her face and she knew . . .

She shot Nick a furious demanding glance—surely he would say something, explain that he had slept next door? But no . . . He sat, his shirt hanging open, his dark hair mussed from sleep, a smug, self-satisfied grin on his handsome, un-shaven face. Then, as though deliberately underlining Iris's assumption that they had slept together, one strong brown hand slid with casual familiarity along the coverlet, outlining the length of Abby's thigh. She stiffened in instant reaction, and would have slapped his hand away except for the presence of Jonathan and Iris. She dared not cause a scene . . .

'Come along, little boy, I'll take you to get some breakfast while your mummy and daddy get dressed.'

For a moment Jonathan hesitated. 'Is he really my daddy?' he asked. His large, innocent eyes clung to his mummy's, demanding the truth.

'Yes, love, really,' Abby confirmed gently. She had no other choice. Nick had seen to that.

As soon as they had left, Abby swung her legs over the opposite side of the bed to Nick, taking the sheet with her and wrapping it around her shoulders like a cloak. 'How could you do that?' she fumed.

'Really you should thank me.' Nick smiled, standing up and facing her across the wide expanse of the bed. His grey eyes lit with laughter at her mutinous expression. 'Look at it this way, Abby darling—by tonight all your friends will know about us. Michael last night and Iris this morning will waste no time in spreading the news to anyone who is interested, and so save you the trouble of explaining.'

She was forced to see the truth of his words. Perhaps it was for the best, she thought bleakly; at least it saved her having to lie to her friends . . .

CHAPTER SIX

IT WAS a warm autumn morning. The rustling leaves of the lofty beech trees guarding the entrance drive to the tiny church were already turning a rich russet-gold. A few lay scattered over the path and crunched under Abby's feet as she walked slowly towards the entrance porch. Iris's steadying hand at her elbow created the only spot of warmth in her whole body. She felt encased in ice, numb with the speed at which the events of the past week had overtaken her.

For days she had battled with a host of unenviable emotions. At first Jonathan had been very wary around his father, listening to his explanation of having to live over the sea and his descriptions of Greece with doubtful acceptance. He had clung more than usual to Abby, until with one simple act Nick had won him over.

The wheel had come off his favourite truck for the umpteenth time, and Nick had hustled the boy into his car along with the broken truck and taken him to a real garage to get it repaired. When the pair of them had returned to the gallery two hours later, Jonathan had been full of his outing and had shown Abby with great pride the newly soldered wheel of his toy. Then, with typical male chauvinism, he had remarked in a lordly manner, 'You see, Mummy, you need men for mechanical things. Daddy told me so.'

She had been consumed by jealousy, used to having Jonathan depend on her for everything; it had hurt to see him standing quite happily with his father's arm around his shoulders.

Nick had had the same success with Iris. Turning on the charm like a water fountain, he had Iris convinced that he was the best thing since sliced bread. Harry had been equally as gullible, while Abby had been forced to listen with mounting horror and hurt as Nick had arranged for the

90

wedding to take place in the private church at Trevlyn Cove.

A tug at her sleeve brought her back to the present. Iris, looking lovely in a pale blue suit that exactly matched the blue of her eyes, was staring at her with deep concern.

'Are you all right, dear? You were miles away.'

'No . . . yes, I'm fine,' she responded tautly, forcing a smile to her frozen lips. The porch was a mass of golden chrysanthemums—Nick's doing, no doubt, she thought bitterly. She smoothed her hands down her thighs in a nervous gesture. The slim-fitting straight cream wool skirt and the matching fitted jacket, with a deep peplum that dipped at the back, were a designer label, another of Nick's choices.

She raised a hand to her throat, the ice-cold feel of the emeralds at her neck reminding her of the bitter argument she had had with him the previous evening.

It had been late, and she had been sitting in her darkened living-room, trying to bring some order to her chaotic mind. Nick had left as usual as soon as Jonathan had gone to bed. His actions of the past week had surprised, puzzled and infuriated her. Why was he insisting on a church wedding? A register office had been more than good enough for him the first time . . . His behaviour towards herself she could not fathom. He had not touched her, hadn't put a foot out of line; he was courteous and attentive, and so understanding that she felt like strangling him. At first she told herself it was only because there were other people present, but as each day passed she was forced to admit that that was not the case. The few times they were alone together she delighted in needling him about the past, his family—anything in an attempt to get him to fight with her—but nothing seemed to upset him. He appeared to be genuinely happy, with a kind of inner contentment that nothing she said or did could rattle. She tried to tell herself it was probably because of Jonathan, but deep down she was not so sure, and that worried her.

Then Nick had walked into the room as though he owned the place. 'Sorry for calling so late, but I forgot to give you this.' He had dropped a jewellery box into her lap.

She had last seen it when she had left Greece, and she had never wanted to see it again. The ensuing argument had left her pale and trembling, long after Nick had left.

Abby's hand dropped from her throat, a wry smile twisting her lovely lips. He reckoned it was a symbolic reminder of some of the happiest moments in their previous marriage, and as such he insisted she wear it today. To her the opposite was true. His penchant for giving expensive jewellery reminded her just how fickle he was.

'Abby, for heaven's sake—they're playing the wedding march for the third time!' Perhaps it was something in Abby's expression, but Iris hesitated, her brows drawing together in a deep, concerned frown. 'I love you as if you were my own daughter, Abby, and if you have the slightest doubt about this marriage it's not too late. We can turn around and walk back down the path just as easily as going forward.'

At Iris's words, Abby's lips trembled and a sheen of moisture coated her lovely eyes, but, taking a deep breath, she straightened her shoulders and stepped forward.

'No, I have no doubts. None at all.' And it was true. She walked down the aisle, her arm through Iris's, her head held high. The church was full, every person in Trevlyn Cove a guest at the wedding. These people deserved a chance to preserve their village, their way of life, and she would do everything necessary to make sure they got it . . .

The wedding ceremony was over, and there was no going back. Nick's dark head bent towards her, his grey eyes glittering with triumph and something else she did not recognise or perhaps did not want to acknowledge. His firm, very male lips captured hers, but she was too numb to feel any reaction. When Iris and Harry were the first to congratulate her she smiled brightly; then, stooping, she dropped a swift kiss on the top of the head of a happily beaming Jonathan.

The wedding breakfast was held at Trevlyn House, Harry kindly lending them his home, but Abby was too tense to eat; Nick stayed by her side as though he could not bear to let her out of his sight, playing the besotted bridegroom to perfection. The popping of champagne corks and filling of glasses signalled the commencement of the toast to their future happiness, ably performed by Harry. Abby, downing her second glass of champagne, found the numbness which had enveloped her all morning slowly melting away. Suddenly, as Nick rose to his feet to respond to the toast, his muscular thigh pressed lightly against her side, sending a jolt of electric awareness arcing through her.

She fidgeted uneasily on her seat, and listened with a slow, burning anger to his perfectly delivered speech. A look around the assembled throng told her they believed his flattery and the heartfelt regret at the original misunderstanding that had parted him from his beautiful wife and son. His closing statement—that he intended never to let her go again—had her green eyes flashing to rest warily on his handsome features. Sensing her regard, he turned and smiled down at her, and it was then that she saw the deadly intent lurking in the depths of his silver-grey eyes.

Abby's heart missed a beat, and she took a hasty swallow of wine and looked away. For a second she could have sworn he meant what he had said. He would not let her go a second time. No, she was imagining things. He was a good actor, that was all. She took a more cautious sip of her wine. She was mistaken . . . had to be. He didn't want her, any more than she wanted him . . .

'I think that went off very well, don't you?' Nick remarked blandly, when they at last drove away from the reception.

'Exactly as you planned,' she replied drily. Once, just once, she would love to see the indomitable Nick Kardis come unstuck, but realistically she knew it would probably never happen. He was a powerful man, with an awesome reputation in the business world. Everything he did, he did to perfection. His one flaw was that he was incapable of love.

The sorrow the thought evoked filled her with self-disgust. God knew she was no longer the young bride looking at marriage through rose-tinted spectacles. Life had dealt her some nasty knocks, but she had survived, and grown stronger. She could do the same again, and there was always Jonathan.

She turned round to check on him, securely strapped into the back seat of the car. 'All right, darling?'

'Yes, Mummy, but I wish I'd had some more confetti.'

Abby chuckled. The high spot of his day so far had been throwing confetti all over his parents. 'I think you had quite enough. I can still feel it stuck inside my jacket.' With a startled exclamation she swung back round as Nick's hand settled on her thigh, his long fingers exerting a gentle pressure on her smooth flesh.

'Don't worry, dear. I'll pick every single piece off you tonight, hmm?' His deep-throated laugh, and the mocking glance he shot her, only served to ignite her anger. She had to choke down a biting reply, and content herself with knocking his hand away. She dared not argue with him, not with Jonathan in the car with them.

Nick had no such reservations and, dropping his voice to a husky drawl, he murmured cynically, 'After all, you have left all your lovers behind you. There is solely me to oblige.'

For the rest of the journey Abby refused to speak to Nick. The only conversation was that between parents and child, and by the time they reached the airport and transferred to the Kardis private jet. Abby was completely excluded. Jonathan, ecstatic at his first flight on an aeroplane, had his father's undivided attention. A fact she was grateful for, as her own thoughts were growing more and more fearful.

All week she had ignored Nick's statement that theirs would be a normal marriage, banishing it to the deepest recesses of her mind. Nick's attitude had helped, as he had never by word or deed alluded to it again. Now she sensed a definite change in his behaviour. When their glances accidentally met, he made no attempt to disguise his masculine interest. His grey eyes flicked lazily over her, lingering deliberately on her full breasts, her long legs, with a sensual familiarity she remembered all too well from the past. The next few months suddenly assumed the proportions of a lifetime. She was no longer so sure of her immunity to Nick's sophisticated sexual expertise, and the thought terrified her.

She barely registered their arrival at Corfu, and on the short car ride to the Kardis villa she fought desperately against a rising tide of pure panic. It was only when they stopped outside the massive portico, ablaze with lights, that her courage returned. If there was one place in the world she hated and had never wanted to see again, it was this house, and somehow that fact gave her the strength to follow Nick and Jonathan calmly up the marble steps to the reception committee waiting in the lofty domed entrance hall.

Jonathan, overawed by the size and magnificence of the place, turned back to Abby and grabbed her hand, his little body leaning into hers. Nick, meanwhile, was greeted like the prodigal son.

'Who are all these people, Mummy, and what are they saying?' Jonathan asked, his grey eyes flickering around the room very warily. 'I don't like this place.' Raising one rather grubby finger, he pointed to the wall. 'Those statues. It looks like a churchyard.'

Abby's laughter rang out clear and pure over the chattering Greek voices, and, swinging her son up in her arms, she hugged him tightly. He put his arms around her neck, his small face smiling up into hers, and they shared a precious moment of joy. 'You're right, darling, it does.' This house had always offended her artistic sensibilities, and Jonathan had hit the nail right on the head. Everything about the place was just that little bit over the top. Too ostentatious, a couple of niches too many in the walls, a surfeit of nude statues, a bit too much marble and gold leaf. 'Don't worry, my love, we won't be staying long,' she told him reassuringly, and her words fell into a sudden silence. Then Nick was at her side.

'Come along, Abby, and say hello to everyone, and perhaps share the joke.' The words were said lightly, but one look at his darkly flushed face and she knew he had heard her last comment and was not all pleased.

'Marta,' she greeted the housekeeper coolly. 'It's nice to see you again.' If the older woman recognised the lie, she gave no hint of it.

'Madam. We so happy you back with your son. I prepare the same rooms for you and the little one, so like his father. Also the cold food I make in the dining-room.'

Abby's jaw dropped, her mouth hanging open like a goldfish. It was the first time Marta had spoken in English to her. She had not even realised the woman knew the language . . . Next came Luc, Marta's husband, and he was equally welcoming. Then Catherine, Nick's sister, and her husband, and five children now, Abby counted in amazement—four girls and one boy.

'Abby, my dear. We are so glad to see you and Nick together again, and your lovely son. Please let me take him. You must be worn out from the journey.'

Catherine was the eternal earth-mother type, and Jonathan instantly recognised it and went to her quite happily, and within minutes was scampering around with his newly discovered cousins.

Abby had anticipated a coolly formal reception, the same as it had been in the past, but the welcome by everyone completely floored her. Who would have thought, she mused, that simply producing a child could bring about such a change in attitude? Catherine amazed her. Surely she more than anyone had cause to resent Jonathan's appearance, as it was her family who stood to lose by it? Yet there was no doubting the genuine warmth in her sister-in-law's smile.

The greatest shock of all was Nick's father. With all the hullabaloo it was hard to focus on anything, except Nick's hand firmly clasping her elbow. He was not so happy; she could sense the tension in his tall frame. Was he still angry? But with his other hand he caught Jonathan and led them across the wide expanse of marble floor to the entrance of the dining-room where his father awaited them.

Her green eyes widened in horror at the once powerful man now slumped in a wheelchair, his huge frame shrunk

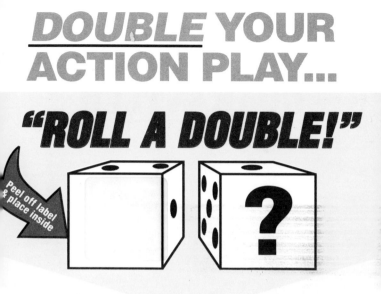

NO RISK, NO OBLIGATION TO BUY...NOW OR EVER!

GUARANTEED

PLAY "ROLL A DOUBLE" AND GET AS MANY AS SIX GIFTS!

HERE'S HOW TO PLAY:

1. Peel off label from front cover. Place it in space provided at right. With a coin, carefully scratch off the silver dice. This makes you eligible to receive one or more free books, and possibly other gifts, depending on what is revealed beneath the scratch-off area.

2. You'll receive brand-new Harlequin Presents® novels. When you return this card, we'll rush you the books and gifts you qualify for ABSOLUTELY FREE!

3. Then, if we don't hear from you, every month we'll send you 6 additional novels to read and enjoy. You can return them and owe nothing, but if you decide to keep them, you'll pay only $2.24 per book—a savings of 51¢ each off the cover price.

4. When you subscribe to the Harlequin Reader Service®, you'll also get our newsletter, as well as additional free gifts from time to time.

5. You must be completely satisfied. You may cancel at any time simply by sending us a note or a shipping statement marked ''cancel'' or by returning any shipment to us at our expense.

You'll look like a million dollars when you wear this elegant necklace! It's a generous 20 inches long and each link is double-soldered for strength and durability.

DETACH AND MAIL CARD TODAY!

HARLEQUIN "NO RISK" GUARANTEE

- You're not required to buy a single book—ever!
- You must be completely satisfied or you may cancel at any time simply by sending us a note or a shipping statement marked "cancel" or by returning any shipment to us at our cost. Either way, you will receive no more books; you'll have no obligation to buy.
- The free book(s) and gift(s) you claimed on this "Roll A Double" offer remain yours to keep no matter what you decide.

If offer card is missing, please write to:
Harlequin Reader Service, 3010 Walden Ave., P.O. Box 1867, Buffalo, N.Y. 14269-1867

DETACH AND MAIL CARD TODAY!

BUSINESS REPLY MAIL
FIRST CLASS MAIL   PERMIT NO. 717   BUFFALO, NY

POSTAGE WILL BE PAID BY ADDRESSEE

HARLEQUIN READER SERVICE
3010 WALDEN AVE
PO BOX 1867
BUFFALO NY 14240-9952

NO POSTAGE
NECESSARY
IF MAILED
IN THE
UNITED STATES

to mere skin and bone. She witnessed with pity, quickly masked, the terrific effort of will it took for him to raise his head and look at her.

'So, Abby, you have finally returned, and with a son. I thank you.' His gnarled hand shook as he reached out and touched Jonathan's black curls, then dropped limply back on to his lap. 'My grandson. A true Kardis. You should not have kept him a secret, Abby.'

The once gimlet eyes, raised to hers, were dull and clouded with pain. Nick's fingers dug into her flesh in silent warning, but it wasn't necessary—she didn't have the heart to argue with the sick old man. Instead she smiled. 'Jonathan and I are pleased to be here. It is good to see you again.'

'Yes, it is good. Enjoy . . . Nurse.' The words were barely above a whisper as his head slumped forward on to his chest.

All Abby's resentment and dislike of her father-in-law disappeared. It was impossible to feel anything but sorrow for the wreck this once proud man had become. It was then she noticed the nurse. The old goat had not changed, she thought with wry amusement. The girl couldn't be more than twenty—dark hair, very beautiful, and very shapely.

In the following few minutes her amusement turned to distaste as she watched the young girl place her hand on Nick's arm and smile softly up at him.

'Nico, it is good you are back,' she offered in a low, husky voice. 'I must get your father back to bed. He should not really be up at all, but he insisted. He refused to allow his grandson to see him for the first time lying in bed.'

Nick's hand dropped from Abby's elbow and, taking the young girl by the arm, he smiled down at her with obvious warmth and affection. 'That's all right, Sophia. I'll see you later.' Then he added casually, 'Oh, by the way, this is my wife, Abby, Sophia Stakis, my father's nurse and family friend.'

I'll just bet she's a family friend, Abby thought cynically.

'Oh, yes,' Abby drawled the words out, not bothering to hide her disgust. The girl looked after the father and slept

with the son, probably. 'Hello.' And with a toss of her red
head she pushed past them, taking Jonathan with her into
the dining-room. The twinge of pain in her stomach, she
was sure, was hunger pangs.

She spent the next five minutes concentrating on getting
Jonathan to eat something from the vast selection of food
set out on the long oak dining table, all the time telling
herself she was glad of the younger woman's presence. It
only confirmed what she already knew; her husband was
an arrogant, despicable swine and the sooner she could get
away from him, the better. . .

Abby popped a morsel of food in her mouth, some kind
of spicy meat wrapped in a vine leaf. It was tasty, but she
wasn't very hungry, and Jonathan, poor soul, was nearly
asleep on his feet. It was way past his usual bedtime.
Suddenly Nick was at her side, Jonathan in his arms, and
he was saying their goodnights to the rest of them. She was
still chewing a mouthful of food as Nick ushered her up the
magnificent marble staircase to their rooms.

She stopped inside the door, a wave of near physical pain
washing over her. Nothing had changed. Her eyes flew to
the huge bed, the scene of her worst humiliation the last
time she was here, and it took all the strength she possessed
to walk into the room. Nick strode past her and straight into
the dressing-room. Coming to her senses, Abby hastily
followed him. 'Wait a minute,' she ordered as Nick lowered
Jonathan on to the single bed. 'I think Jonathan should sleep
with me tonight; after all, this is a strange place to him. He
will sleep better with me.'

Nick straightened up, and his steel-grey eyes clashed
with hers, a derisory anger in their depths. 'No way, Abby.
The boy sleeps here.'

Until that moment she had not really accepted that they
would be sharing a bed, but one look at his harsh face and
she knew it would be futile to argue. Turning on her heel,
she stalked back into the master bedroom and across to the
adjoining bathroom. She was fuming, but also fearful.
Grabbing a face-cloth, she held it under the tap for a
moment, then, squeezing the excess moisture out of it, she

picked up a towel and marched back to the dressing-room. She would show him, she vowed. Not deigning to look at Nick, she sat down on the bed with her son. Quickly she rubbed his face and hands and got him into his pyjamas. He was asleep almost before his head touched the pillow. She leant forward and pressed a soft kiss on his forehead, gently stroking the soft black hair back from his brow.

'Out, Abby. I have something to say to you and I don't want to wake our son,' he commanded grimly.

'Certainly, sir,' she hissed facetiously, and, brushing past him, she strode back into the main bedroom. If he thought she was going to calmly crawl into bed with him, he had another think coming. Defiantly she turned to face him, ready to do battle. She watched him with a burning sense of anger and frustration as he quietly closed the dressing-room door behind him and walked across to stand about a foot away from her. Her glance rested for a moment on his broad shoulders. He had removed his jacket and tie earlier and the expensive white silk shirt he wore was unbuttoned almost to his waist, revealing his tanned, hair-roughened, muscular chest. Her pulse-rate leapt alarmingly and her body's treacherous response only served to fuel her anger. Green eyes flashing, she met and held his icy, intense gaze. 'What do you have to say?' she prompted.

'You are my wife, the mother of my son, and as such deserve my support. But I will not have you behaving disrespectfully to the rest of my family. Is that understood?' he demanded hardily.

She didn't understand. Sure, she had told Jonathan they would not be staying long, but that was hardly insulting. Unless . . . the nurse . . . of course. 'I wasn't aware Sophia was a member of your family. Is she?' she queried mockingly.

'She is under my protection and you deliberately insulted her. I——'

'Oh. Sorry,' she cut in with exaggerated courtesy. Nick reached out and lifted her chin with one long finger, his grey eyes narrowing perceptibly on her flushed face. He was laughing at her.

'You never used to be so bitchy, darling. Jealous, hmm?'

His obvious amusement only served to inflame her anger even more. He was so damn sure of himself.

'Jealous? You must be joking!' she scorned. 'She's welcome to you. At least it will keep you out of my bed.' And with a spirited gesture she brushed his hand away.

'Oh, no,' he denied, sliding his glance up and down the length of her with a sensuous, predatory knowledge that made her skin burn. 'Nobody will keep me out of your bed tonight, and that includes you, my dear Abby.'

'Resorting to rape become a habit, has it?' she derided viciously, in direct reference to the last time they had shared this room together. In the back of her mind was the vain hope that if she could rile him sufficiently he might storm off and leave her alone. For a moment she thought she had succeeded—amusement gave way to icy anger, and his hands clenched and unclenched at his sides. 'What's the matter, Nick? The truth hurt?' she goaded.

'No,' he growled. The tension in the air was a tangible force. She could sense the battle within him to retain his self-control. Then, with a shake of his dark head, he squared his shoulders and turned from her to walk towards the door.

'You wouldn't recognise the truth if it hit you in the face,' he pointed gratingly. 'It was never rape with you and me. Once I took you in anger, but after the first few seconds you were with me all the way. Even so, I am not going to make the same mistake again, so you might as well stop your sniping, Abby. It's not going to work. I refuse to argue with you on our wedding night.'

'You're a swine, Nick,' she choked bitterly, humiliatingly aware that she could not refute his statement.

'Maybe. But tonight I'm going to do the gentlemanly thing.'

Abby's hand shot up and she stared at Nick, her green eyes wide with mingled surprise and hope. 'You mean . . . ?'

'I mean you can use the bathroom first. I have to check on my father. I won't be long . . .' he drawled suggestively.

She could still hear the echo of his laughter long after he had left the room. He wasn't a swine—'fiend' was a better word, she fumed as she stormed into the bathroom.

The en-suite did not have a lock—obviously it had not been considered necessary in a master bedroom—but the omission made Abby strip off at once and take the quickest shower of her life. It was stupid, she knew, Nick was not likely to intrude on her ablutions, but she was taking no chances. She wrapped a bathtowel around her slender body and, bundling her clothes into a heap, she sped across the bedroom, quietly entering the dressing-room where her son slept.

At the foot of the bed was the suitcase she had opened earlier to find his pyjamas; there had been no time to unpack properly. She rooted around until she found a large white T-shirt, her usual night attire, and, dropping the towel carelessly to the floor, she dragged the T-shirt over her head. With one last look at the sleeping boy, she silently left the room. Dashing across the bedroom, she switched off the lights and scrambled inelegantly in to the huge, ornately carved bed. With luck she would be fast asleep before Nick returned.

It was silly, she knew; she was acting like a terrified virgin, but she didn't seem able to help it. God! She knew Nick's body as intimately as her own; they had already been lovers, man and wife. It was mad to be so afraid.

Curling up into a little ball, her knees almost on her chest, Abby lay on the very edge of the bed, the covers pulled up under her chin and her hand clenched around the side of the mattress. Sternly she berated herself. She was being ridiculous. She was a mature woman. She could accept Nick's lovemaking without a qualm. No, not lovemaking. Sex. That was the operative word. She had to remember it could only ever be sex. She would take a leaf out of Nick's book. Sex was an enjoyable appetite not to be denied. Only the young and naïve thought of it as love. So long as she remembered that, she could get through the next few months emotionally unscathed. Satisfied with her new mature logic, she began to relax.

She yawned widely and snuggled deeper into the soft bed. She was worn out and so very tired. Her fingers slowly unclenched on the edge of the mattress, only to grip it again even tighter than before at the sound of the door opening. Her whole body froze, locked with tension. Nick was back . . . She forced herself to breathe deeply and evenly, feigning sleep, but she could not blot out the muffled sounds Nick made preparing for bed. With eyes closed tightly, she listened with steadily rising agitation to the sound of the shower running and her heartbeat accelerated alarmingly when it stopped. The very silence was threatening . . .

Abby felt a rush of cold air across her back, and the mattress depress. She lay perfectly still, almost holding her breath, then a large hand clasped her shoulder and her body went rigid.

'Stop pretending you're asleep, Abby,' Nick's breath whispered in her ear.

A convulsive shiver skidded down her spine and she was mortified that he had seen through her pretence so easily. Even so, she was not about to admit it, and, making a small whimpering sound, she slowly opened her eyes. 'Mmm? Wh-what?' she queried with fake puzzlement, but Nick was not about to let her get away with it.

The hand tightened on her shoulder, and callously he leant across her and switched on the bedside light, then deliberately forced her on to her back.

'Not what, Abby—who! I want you to see who it is making love to you. There will be no pretending I'm Harkness or any other of your lovers, understand?' he warned ominously.

Reluctantly she met his eyes, and flinched at the cynical intent reflected in their molten depths. She would not fight him; she would not give him the satisfaction of overpowering her. Let him do his worst, but he would find a frigid woman in his arms, she vowed silently.

'Surely no woman could mistake the touch of the great Nick Kardis?' she sneered, sarcasm her only defence against the subtle assault on her senses that his nearness aroused.

His dark eyes flashed angrily before resuming their more

usual amused mockery. Slowly he lowered his head, balancing his weight on his forearms either side of her so she was encaged in the circle of his supremely masculine body. 'It won't work, Abby. I told you before that I refuse to argue with you tonight. I have something much more pleasurable in mind,' he drawled silkily.

She felt his warm breath on her face, and, unable to withstand the sensuous promise in his eyes, she let her gaze skid to his wide shoulders, which were gleaming gold in the subdued lighting. She drew a shaky breath, a shudder coursing through her as she realised he was completely naked, his long length pressing against her, burning through the thin cotton of her T-shirt.

'And I don't really think you want me to,' he mocked, recognising her body's involuntary response. 'You're a very passionate lady, and you've been celibate for at least a week.'

It was pride alone that gave her the courage to bait him. 'A week? You can't know that. We only met again last Sunday.' God! If he ever found out she had never had another lover, how he would gloat! She felt the tension in his huge frame, his anger a palpable emotion. Why it should be, she could not begin to understand. He did not pretend to love her, so what did it matter how many men she had slept with? But it did bother him and she was glad, glad that in some small way she could hurt him. Bravely she raised her eyes to his face. His features were etched in sharp relief, the tanned skin pulled taut across every plane and hollow. A pulse jerked spasmodically in his jaw as she watched him battle with his fury . . . and win.

'Good try, Abby,' he rasped, his dark gaze unwavering on her lovely face. 'But it won't work. When I ultimately take possession of your luscious body it will be because you've asked me to, I promise. And as for the rest, I arrived in St Ives last Saturday night and watched your rather passionate doorstep farewell with Harkness. He left a hungry man, not a satiated one.'

Shaken by his evocative promise and his revelation that he had calmly watched her in the arms of another man, she

could only stare up at him, a feeling of helplessness
overtaking her. Melanie had been right about everything, it
seemed.

'It doesn't even bother you that I hate you?' She
murmured the words more to herself than to him. Even now,
after all that had happened between them, she still found it
incredible he could be so lacking in conscience.

'No. Why should it? You're in my bed. What more could
I want? And you're much too lovely to fight with.' He
smiled mockingly and bent his head.

She felt his lips on her throat, and she jerked her head
away, shocked by her own leaping response to his lightest
caress. His mouth closed over the fast-beating pulse in her
throat and she shivered as he slid one strong hand insolently
over her shoulder, her breast, the curve of her waist and
thigh, and then back again to linger tantalisingly, cupping
her breast. She felt her nipple harden beneath his palm, the
traitorous response of her body to his touch a bitter
humiliation to her. 'I don't want this,' she gasped.

Nick merely laughed and she shuddered as his hand
squeezed gently on her breast.

'Yes, you do, sweetheart,' he drawled silkily, before his
lips closed over hers, his heavy body pinning her to the bed.

The brush of his lips on her mouth was as soft and gentle
as a butterfly wing; his lips teased hers again and again, like
a bee sipping nectar from a flower, and her resistance
crumbled to nothing. Afterwards she told herself that if he
had used force she would never have given in so easily, but
Nick was much too clever for that.

His tongue flicked lightly around her mouth, enticing a
fluttering response she was powerless to withhold. He went
on kissing her, parting her trembling lips, his tongue
delving deep until she ardently returned his kisses, and
when he deliberately drew back a soft sigh of regret escaped
her.

'You want me,' he said, his silver eyes staring down into
hers. 'And God knows, I want you. You were mine first and
you will be mine last and forever.' With a hint of hardness
in his voice he added, 'I am going to imprint myself on you,

body and soul, so that never again will you look at another man.'

Abby lay immobile, trapped by the sensuous delight her body had been denied for far too long, and, worse, by a tiny voice in the darkest reaches of her consciousness that said yes to his domination. 'No!' she cried, in denial of the traitorous inner voice more than of Nick's statement.

'Yes, yes,' he mocked her, and with a deftness that underlined his vast experience he removed her T-shirt and dropped it on the floor. 'If that was meant to put me off, Abby, it didn't work,' he growled softly, his glittering, omniscient gaze studying her now naked body with lazy pleasure. 'You were always beautiful, but now you are unbelievably lovely—perfect.' His gaze lingered on her full breasts before lifting to her flushed face.

Abby felt her whole body blush, heat racing through her. Her green eyes skated helplessly over his handsome face—noting the darkening flush across his high cheekbones, the sensuous twist to his full lips—and on down to the broad expanse of his muscular chest, the curling black body hair arrowing down to his navel, and lower. Her heart thudded in her breast. She was bewitched by the sheer masculine perfection of him, just as she had been years ago. Desperately she closed her eyes, and repeated in her mind: it is only sex, just sex.

'No, Abby, don't close your eyes.' One long finger with a feather-night touch traced along her collarbone in a familiar path to her burgeoning breast. 'I want you to see what I'm doing to you,' Nick drawled throatily. 'And what you do to me.'

She willed herself not to respond, but it was hopeless. The husky sound of his voice alone aroused goose-bumps all over her, never mind anything else, and when his thumb trailed oh, so lightly over the tips of her breasts, her body arched involuntarily towards the source of its pleasure. With long fingers he circled her navel and lower to the softly curling feminine hair at the apex of her thighs. A low moan escaped her; she was lost and she knew it.

'Open your eyes, Abby, sweet, sweet Abby.' The throaty

incantation was a command she could not resist as his hard-muscled thigh gently nudged her trembling legs apart, and he moved to cover her completely.

Naked bodies, touching from shoulder to thigh. A slow, burning ache started in her stomach; moist heat flooded her loins as his teasing fingers found the secret parts of her. The musky male scent of him enveloped her and helplessly she gazed up at him, her green eyes wide and hazed with passion.

'Good,' he breathed into her mouth, his dark eyes glittering with fierce triumph. Her soft lips parted, and his mouth took hers in a kiss of deep, savage possession. 'You're mine,' he rasped, breaking the kiss to trail a tongue of flame down her throat.

'Yes, oh, yes,' Abby sighed as his mouth closed over the rigid peak of her breast. With tongue and teeth he tormented first one and then the other, and all the while his hands continued to caress her quivering flesh. Whimpering sounds of pleasure escaped her as passion spiralled and consumed her. Her hands tangled in the black silk hair of his head, holding him to her, while her long legs entwined themselves around his. She could feel the rigid length of his masculine arousal hard against her, and the sheer intensity of his throbbing desire blotted out her every thought.

Nothing existed for Abby but Nick. It had been so long, so very long since his hands had touched her this way . . . His mouth teased, and tasted, burning where he touched, and the feelings she had denied for years surged through her body like a dam breaking, and she was swept away on a mindless tide of passion. His tongue licked over the flat plane of her stomach, his large hands gripping her thighs, his mouth hot, moist against her quivering flesh. Her body arched like a bowstring at the most intimate caress of all.

Abby grasped his head between her trembling hands and urged his mouth to hers. She wanted to feel his full possession, needed to . . . 'Now, now,' she moaned, her hands sliding to grasp his broad shoulders, her nails digging into his flesh in her need.

'Yes, Abby, yes,' he gentled her, as his hands curved

under her buttocks, and with one fierce thrust they were joined as one. In seconds she was lost in a shuddering, convulsive climax that they reached in perfect unison. Nick's harsh groans mingled with her keening cry of ecstatic release.

Nick rolled slowly off her, and Abby felt strangely bereft. The only sound in the room was their heavy, laboured breathing. God! How could she have denied her own sexuality for so long? she thought in wonder, and was immediately flooded with shame at her own wanton behaviour.

'So now we know,' Nick rasped, and pulled her into the curve of his shoulder. He lifted a hand and smoothed back the tangled mass of red hair from her brow in an oddly gentle gesture. 'The chemistry is still as strong as ever, hmm?'

Abby didn't answer—she didn't dare, not even to herself—and, closing her eyes, she slept.

CHAPTER SEVEN

ABBY'S sleep was haunted by dreams. She moaned, threshing restlessly on the bed, her body burning, aching for release. Only she wasn't dreaming. Three times in the night she awakened, aroused and wanting, floating mindless with desire, and willingly she accepted Nick's passionate kisses, his aggressive, thrusting domination. The first rays of the morning sun were slanting across the wide bed when she finally found the deep sleep her body needed, safely wrapped in the arms of her husband . . .

Slowly she opened her eyes, the sound of childish screams and laughter ringing in her ears. She yawned and stretched languorously, then as languor gave way to reality she shot off the bed. A quick glance told her Nick was long gone, and without considering her naked state she went straight to Jonathan's room. The bed was made, the suitcases nowhere in sight; she opened a wardrobe door and there were all her clothes. She might have guessed. Marta must have unpacked, and the sounds floating in from the balcony window were evidence of her son's whereabouts. With a groan of dismay she quickly grasped a pair of lacy briefs and a pair of cream cotton trousers with a matching cream checked shirt, and hurried back into the main bedroom. A swift glance at the bedside clock made her close her eyes in shame. God! It was almost noon. What on earth would everyone think? Some mother, no doubt, and the rest . . .

Damn Nick, damn him to hell! she thought bitterly, striding across the room to the en-suite. How he must be gloating. She had succumbed to him just as she always had in the past. Standing under the shower, she turned the water on full blast, then with methodical precision she scrubbed every inch of her skin in a vain attempt to wash away his every touch. It was a futile gesture, but at least it made her feel slightly better.

She got dried and dressed quickly. Returning to the dressing-room, she found a pair of tan loafers and slipped them on her feet. It was only when she sat down at the dressing-table and began to brush the tangles out of her flowing mane of hair that she dared to think about the previous night.

A stiffness in her muscles, a soreness in tender places reminded her all too well of just how passionately she had responded to her husband's lovemaking. No—no, she told herself, not lovemaking . . . sex. She supposed she should be grateful to Nick—at least he had not insulted her intelligence by saying he loved her, something he had done all the time in the past, when she had been green enough to believe him. A heavy sigh escaped her as she put the brush down. So much for the old adage that sex without love was no good. Her own innate honesty forced her to admit it wasn't true in her case—or Nick's. He had taken her to the heights and beyond with a sexual expertise she could only marvel at. Yet she did not love him and he certainly didn't love her. She didn't even like him . . .

Rooting through her handbag, she found a couple of hair-grips and slid one behind each ear to hold back her tumbling curls. She eyed her reflection with distaste. Her face looked softer somehow, her full lips still swollen from Nick's kisses. He had won again. His family would take one look at her and presume everything was back to normal, the happily married couple. Just what Nick wanted. Squaring her shoulders, she breathed deeply and stood up; the ache in her heart she ignored along with all her other aching muscles.

The villa was a huge rambling sort of sugar-plum castle with everything in it. All the main rooms looked out over formal gardens with a large patio and swimming-pool. A tree-lined walkway led down to the edge of a cliff where stone steps were cut into the rock down to a small beach and the sea. Oddly enough, Abby could not remember ever going on the beach. No one seemed to use it, and the one time she had suggested it to Nick in the past he had said no, the pool was better, and in those days she had never argued with him.

She stood at the back of the patio unnoticed for a moment. Jonathan and all the other children were in the pool, and sitting at a large white table, coffee-cups in front of them, were Nick and his sister, watching the children in the water. Late October in Corfu was still warm, and Nick was wearing only brief black swimming-trunks. She stared at his lithe brown figure and her heart skipped a beat as a vivid picture of their naked bodies entwined flashed in her mind. She cringed inwardly at the thought of how she had so humiliatingly surrendered to the passions he had aroused in her, but looking at him, the sun gleaming on his golden, smooth-muscled body, she consoled herself with the thought that the woman hadn't been born who could resist him—he was a picture of sheer masculine perfection.

She must have made a sound. As Nick turned and caught her staring, he smiled broadly and stood up. Abby moved forward, furious with herself at being caught watching him, but in a couple of lithe strides Nick was standing in front of her, his near naked body blocking her view of the rest of them.

'Abby. You slept well, hmm?' he asked. His grey eyes smiled knowingly into hers and she blushed.

'You should have woken me up—Jonathan needs me in the morning,' she hissed, and, ignoring the hand he raised to detain her, she pushed past him and sat down at the table.

'Good morning, Abby.' Catherine greeted her with a broad grin. 'So you've finally surfaced. If you don't mind I will leave you and big brother here to look after the children, I have some things to do. Help yourself to coffee—it is fresh.' And with that she got up and went back into the house.

Grateful for something to do, Abby pulled a clean cup towards her and filled it with coffee. She took a deep swallow of the refreshing liquid and, with a nonchalance she did not feel, looked around the pool, ignoring Nick as he slid into the chair opposite her. A small smile tugged the corner of her mouth as she recognised Jonathan totally engrossed in showing Catherine's son the rudiments of life-saving. Thank God they were sitting on the bottom of the pool in only a foot of water.

'Abby, it's no good pretending I'm not here. Perhaps I should have awakened you earlier, but I thought you needed to sleep and, contrary to what you may think, I am quite capable of looking after my own son. In fact, I rather enjoyed it,' he opined reasonably, and, leaning forward, he covered her hand where it lay on the table with his much larger one.

The sensual warmth of his touch triggered an immediate response in her that filled her with dismay and a rising anger. Hastily she jerked her hand away, and, cradling her cup in both hands, she raised it to her lips and drained it. Replacing it on the table, she took a deep calming breath and raised her head. Green eyes clashed with grey, and for a second she was stunned by the tenderness in Nick's expression, but then he had always been a great actor, she told herself. 'You might find it an amusing diversion to attend to your son once in a while, but it happens to be my job permanently and you should have allowed Jonathan to waken me. Unless of course you intended to give your family the impression I'm an inept mother, lying in bed all morning,' she opined curtly.

'Don't be ridiculous, Abby. I——'

'I'm not being ridiculous, just stating a fact,' she cut him off sharply. His grey eyes narrowed assessingly on her mutinous face, and it took all her self-control to withstand his scrutiny.

'My family are not so uncaring as to expect a newly wedded bride to be up at the crack of dawn the first day of her marriage, but that is not the real reason you're as prickly as a hedgehog this morning, is it, my sweet Abby?' he drawled softly.

He knew exactly what was bothering her, the swine, and she longed to knock the easy smile off his handsome face, but, considering where they were, and the children, she did not dare. Instead she gritted her teeth and responded coldly, 'I don't know what you mean, and I don't think I want to know.' Hardly the brightest come-back in the world, but all she could think of. She had forgotten just how intimidating Nick could be. He had stood up and walked around the table; with one hand on the back of her chair and the other on the table in front of her, he leant over her so her eyes were on a level with his naked, hair-roughened chest. She lowered her gaze, but that was worse, as her eyes rested on his narrow waist and slim hips, his taut thighs and long legs planted slightly apart. The musky male scent of him enveloped her and she wished he had some clothes on. It was the lesser evil to tilt her head back and face him.

'Stop hating yourself, Abby. You're my wife—love-making between you and me was always great. It is no sin to admit you enjoyed last night.' Straightening slightly, he lifted his hand from the table and trailed one long finger around the swollen outline of her mouth. 'I know I did,' he husked throatily.

She knew he was going to kiss her, and, jerking away from him, she snapped, 'Don't touch me!' Her chair crashed to the ground as she stood up. 'And as for last night, lovemaking didn't come into it. It was sex . . . pure and simple.' Her nerves were stretched to breaking-point in her effort to pretend last night had not affected her. Viciously sarcastic, she added, 'Sex. That is all, and no one would quarrel with your expertise, but then you have had plenty of practice.'

The smile left his face, and if she hadn't known him better she would have thought he was in pain, but then his steel-grey eyes narrowed to mere slits. The air was electric with tension, a nerve twitched in his jaw and Abby had the sinking sensation she had gone too far.

'Sex,' he drawled silkily. 'Of course, I was forgetting you are no longer the innocent I first married, but a woman of experience . . . How remiss of me.' And in one swift move he pulled her into his arms.

He held her tight against his near naked body with one arm while his mouth crashed down on hers in a kiss that drove all the air from her body. He did not stop until she was trembling helplessly in his arms. The feel of his muscular thighs against her slender legs burnt through the thin fabric of her trousers. He slid his hands to her buttocks and pressed her into the cradle of his hips, making her blatantly aware of his hard masculine arousal.

'Sex, you say,' he snarled. 'Well, I don't remember ever wanting or asking for anything else, my dear wife. But you would do well not to deride it.' And with insulting ease he lifted one hand to close over her breast; his long fingers found her nipple and teased it to instant rigidity. Grasping her by the shoulders, he thrust her away from him and with a knowing, derisory glance he stared at her full breasts, the tips outlined in hard relief against the soft cotton of her shirt.

'I despise you,' she choked, but she could not look at him, too ashamed of her own reaction.

'Despise me as much as you like,' he sneered. 'But when it comes to . . . sex,' he flicked her breast with a callous finger, 'we both know you can't say no.'

Abby shivered beneath his icy, contemptuous gaze. To deny the truth of his words would be useless; her body would betray the lie. Bile rose in her throat and threatened to choke her. How dared he treat her with contempt? Contempt should be her prerogative. He had stormed back into her contented life and turned it upside-down, all for money and power.

From deep within her, the anger, the resentment that had been bubbling inside her all week spilled forth in a vitriolic attack. 'How dare you look down your arrogant Greek nose at me? When we both know you have never said no to anything in a skirt in your life. You're a sly, conniving chauvinist pig who thinks nothing of cheating his own sister's f——'

'Shut up, just shut up!' he hissed through clenched teeth, his lips ringed white with rage. 'Remember where you are.'

'Mummy, Daddy, are you fighting?'

Abby closed her eyes. She had forgotten the children. Opening her eyes, she looked down into Jonathan's upturned face, a worried frown marring his usually happy features.

'No, darling. It's all right. We were pretending, that's all.' And, dropping to her haunches, she gathered his wet, squirming, near naked body into her arms. 'I'm sorry I wasn't awake to get you dressed this morning,' she murmured, kissing his soft cheek.

'That's all right. Daddy helped, and guess what, Mummy? I had breakfast with lots of people. I have five cousins and an aunty and uncle and lots of relations.' Then, pulling out of her arms, he looked up at Nick. 'Isn't that right, Daddy?' he asked, begging his father's confirmation of this amazing state of affairs.

Abby straightened, shooting a wary look at Nick. Was his anger going to extend to her son? No . . . His hard face relaxed into a genuine smile as he ruffled Jonathan's wet hair with an affectionate hand.

'Yes, it's true, son, and who knows? In time you might even have a brother or sister as well.' His eyes met hers over the top of the little boy's head, his smile turning to a cynical sneer as he registered her horror-stricken expression. Jonathan, hearing his name called, ran back to the pool, all interest in the conversation forgotten, while Abby felt as if she had been kicked in the stomach.

'No need to look so shaken, Abby. Given your lust for sex and your lifestyle of the past few years, no doubt you're guarded against any unwanted pregnancy, hmm?'

A hollow laugh escaped her and, luckily for her, Nick took it as confirmation of his surmise, and with a muttered curse he turned and joined the children in the pool.

She sank down into the nearest chair, appalled by her own stupidity. Abby had never considered the possibility of getting pregnant again, but now it occupied her whole mind. There was no excuse. At her age she should know better than to go to bed with a man without the protection of birth control. For months the television at home had run a campaign against unprotected sex. Even the youngest teenager was more aware than she had been. Why? Why had she been so blind . . .? She tried to convince herself it would be all right. After all, it had taken well over a year for her to conceive last time. Perhaps it wasn't too late, if somehow she could get to see a doctor and obtain a prescription for the Pill . . . It wasn't too late . . . It couldn't be . . .

Without conscious thought, she stood up and walked away from the pool and down into the garden. Strolling between the long avenue of almond trees that led to the rocky headland, she told herself over and over again that she had nothing to worry about. In a few months she would be free to leave Nick, and nothing would prevent her, she vowed, but a perverse, tiny part of her felt regret. It would have been nice for Jonathan to have a brother or sister, a little baby . . . She squashed the image before it could form. Not with Nick as the father. Never again . . .

Abby breathed deeply of the hot, scented air, some semblance of calm returning to her. She looked around her, drinking in the beauty of her surroundings. The sea gleamed emerald-green traced with silver as it chased along the rocks of the tiny cove below. The house was situated on the north west coast of the island, not far from Aghios Stefanos, and to Abby's mind the most beautiful part of Corfu. Durrell's world of romantic little bays, portrayed so lovingly in *Prospero's Cell*.

She turned to walk back towards the house and her lips twitched in the beginnings of a smile as a long-forgotten memory surfaced in her mind. Behind the house the hills rose steep and wooded. It had been the eleventh of August, the first year of her marriage and a festival for St Spiridon, the patron saint of the island, and a big percentage of all the male population, it seemed to Abby, were called Spiros after him. The villa had been crowded with guests and Nick had insisted after lunch they slip away for a walk. They had walked miles inland—it probably was not all that far, but as it was all uphill it had seemed so at the time. Eventually they had collapsed together under the shade of a huge, gnarled oak tree, and there in the open they had stripped each other naked and made slow, passionate love. It had been afterwards the fun had started, as in funny . . . Nick had been wearing only a pair of much-loved faded blue jeans, and when they had finally decided to get dressed the jeans were nowhere to be found. Until Abby spotted some hundred yards up the hill a disreputable-looking shaggy goat with huge horns firmly wrapped in a pair of blue jeans.

She had laughed until the tears had rolled down her cheeks as Nick, naked as a jay bird, had chased the animal for over half an hour before he'd finally recovered the tattered remnants of his jeans.

It was Jonathan's high-pitched yell of, 'Mummy, lunch!' that brought her back to the present, and with a shiver of unease she ascended the steps to the patio. She was shocked to realise that in the past few years she had never allowed a happy memory of her previous marriage to surface—only the horror of the last few months before the divorce had she kept in the forefront of her mind—but now she was married again and on this beautiful island, happier memories were invidiously returning to haunt her, and she didn't like it. Not one bit . . . Her delicately arched brows drew together in a worried frown. She hated Nick . . . didn't she? That was all she needed to remember. He would not get under her skin a second time. No way . . .

Abby almost laughed out loud at her fears as she looked around the table. Everyone was seated and waiting for her—Catherine and Theo with their children, Jonathan with a vacant seat next to him—but Nick was seated at the head of the large, oblong table with Sophia the nurse at his elbow, deep in conversation and oblivious to Abby's presence. Abby had nothing to worry about. Nick no more wanted to get involved seriously with her than she did with him . . .

Lunch was a prolonged affair, and Abby took little part in the conversation but allowed it to flow over her. Nick made one remark directly to her and that was near the end of the meal, and only she knew he was mocking her when he solicitously informed her, 'You must excuse me this afternoon, my dear, but I have an appointment with the family lawyer in Corfu Town. I'm sure you understand.' And, rising from the table, he left, as Abby choked down the bitter rejoinder that leapt to her tongue. My God! He could not even wait a day to make sure the will was changed, bothering the poor lawyer on a Sunday . . .

It was with this thought in mind that she made no comment when, later over coffee, Catherine broke into a long-winded eulogy on Nick's goodness, ending with the assertion, 'I'm sure you and Nick will make a go of it this time. When you left before, it was as though a light went out inside of him, he missed you so dreadfully.'

Abby choked on a mouthful of coffee. 'You're joking!' she exclaimed before she could stop herself, then squirmed under the reproachful look in Catherine's big brown eyes.

'It was no joke to us who had to watch him. Oh, he tried to hide it—he has worked twenty-hour days for years, and made us all even wealthier—but I know my brother. All the vitality, his love of life had deserted him. It was painful to see, and he would allow no one near him to help him, until a few weeks ago when he discovered he had a son. It was like a miracle—he was so happy when he told me about you and Jonathan—I wept with joy.'

Abby did not doubt the sincerity of her sister-in-law's words, but she cringed at the misplaced loyalty. The poor woman obviously had no idea about the business and the terms of her father's will—Nick had fooled her, the same as he had everyone else.

She bit down on her resentment as Catherine continued with, 'I'm not blaming you for leaving Nick—I'm not blind to his faults and I can understand why you thought you had to go. But I do think you were hasty.'

'Hasty?' Abby prompted. After all she had put up with!

'Yes, hasty. You should have told him you were pregnant. It would have made all the difference in the world to him to know you were having a child.'

'Would it?' Abby remarked cynically, longing to tell her the truth, but she could not bring herself to disillusion the woman.

'Yes. I know the papers were saying unkind things about him at the time, but Nick is a powerful man and very newsworthy. There will always be stories about him—it is one of the drawbacks of being a man in his position. He loves children, and now he has you and Jonathan back I'm sure everything will be fine.'

There was no answer to that, Abby thought wryly. Her sister-in-law's view of Nick was so totally opposed to her

own, but then Catherine was Greek, and, according to Nick,
very like his mother. She would probably condone a
mistress or two without batting an eyelid.

Abby took a last look in the mirror, and flicked one errant
red curl of hair with a nervous hand. She had spent the last
few hours playing with the children, supervising their
evening meal and finally putting Jonathan to bed. Now,
dressed in a slim blue silk sheath and carefully made-up,
she was ready to go downstairs and join the rest of the adults
for dinner. It was almost nine, and Nick had not yet
returned. She did not know whether to be glad or sorry; all
she did know was that her stomach was tying itself in knots
at the thought of the night ahead.

She had almost reached the bottom of the ornate marble
staircase when Nick dashed in. She hesitated, her hand
gripping the banister as he strolled towards her, his grey
eyes shining appreciatively as he subjected her to a
lightning appraisal.

'Very lovely, darling. Have you missed me? Or shouldn't
I ask?'

Hurrying on down, she snapped, 'Like a hole in the
head!' angry at her stupidly racing pulse.

He threw his head back and laughed out loud. 'That's my
girl. Honest to a fault in some things.' And before she knew
what he was about, he had grabbed her around the waist and
pulled her hard against his long body. 'But where it matters,
not so truthful, hmm?' His mouth crushed down on hers and
she reeled under the impact. 'Sex, only sex,' he mocked. 'I
wonder . . .'

For an instant she almost succumbed to the laughing
invitation in his grey eyes, vividly reminded of a younger,
carefree Nick. But from somewhere she found the strength
to withstand him.

'Obviously your business went well. Does that mean we
can leave here?' she asked coldly. A shutter seemed to drop
over his face as she spoke, his expression suddenly
hard.

'Yes, my business is concluded, and we will leave

tomorrow.'

'For Cornwall?' she prompted. Well, there was no harm in trying.

'No . . . for Athens and your new home,' he informed her curtly, and, turning, ascended the stairs.

Dinner was a sombre affair, which was not surprising under the circumstances. The sole topic of conversation was the elder Mr Kardis and his failing health. Abby wasn't required to say much, and for that she was grateful. She had spent half an hour earlier with the old man, and she had grave doubts that he would last even a few months. The thought made her feel terribly guilty, and gave her another reason to curse Nick. It was all his fault she was in this ambivalent position, her own freedom depending on someone else's demise.

The dinner conversation did reveal one fact Abby had not been aware of. The villa was now Catherine's and her husband's permanent home, and had been for over two years. Seemingly they had given up their home in Athens when their fourth child had been born, and had moved out here. Abby did not like the house, but it still surprised her that Nick had allowed his sister to have it. He wasn't the sort to let go of anything . . . That thought disturbed her for quite another reason, and she was thankful when Nick excused himself to visit his father. She said a hasty goodnight to everyone and went straight to bed, hopefully to sleep before her husband arrived. But it was a futile hope . . .

The next morning Abby awoke early, but even so Nick had already left their bed. She turned her head into the pillow and groaned in self-disgust. Once again she had given in to his sophisticated erotic expertise, following blindly where he led until she had ended up begging him to take her. She despised the kind of man he was, but once in his arms, his hard male body hot against her own, every sensible thought flew and she was defeated, engulfed in feelings she could not control.

She cringed at her own naïveté, her stupid conceit. When they had met again after so many years, she had actually

convinced herself that seeing him again had set her free.
Free to enjoy another man's caress, ready and willing to
resume an active emotional life. What a fool she had been.
She could see now that it was Nick's presence, and his
alone, that had awakened her long-dormant feminine
desires. God! Was she doomed to spend the rest of her life
responding only to Nick? The thought was chilling.

Her delight after going out with Ian and kissing him,
enjoying his embrace, seemed totally foolish to her now.
Her reaction to Ian paled into insignificance when she
considered the storm of emotions her ruthless husband
aroused in her.

Sliding her long legs over the side of the bed, she stood
up and, picking her robe off the foot of the bed, slipped it
on and tied the belt firmly around her narrow waist. Her
only consolation, she thought wearily as she padded
barefoot across to Jonathan's room, was that at least this
time she had no illusions about love. Oddly enough, she
recalled enough about the past to realise that, although she
shared the most intimate act with Nick, it was not quite the
same as before, and that was some comfort. She no longer
gave quite everything. There was some small part of her
that remained untouched. Some little bit of her mind, her
heart that remained inviolate. A constant voice that
subconsciously reminded her that Nick was not to be
trusted. Not worthy of love . . .

'Will you hurry up, Abby? We want to leave today, not
tomorrow,' Nick's deep voice called sarcastically across the
foyer.

Abby, with a last hug for Catherine and a wave to the
assembled children, dashed down the steps to the waiting
car. She slid into the back seat, and found herself sitting not
next to Jonathan but to Sophia. She choked back the
question that leapt to her mind. She would be damned if she
would give Nick the satisfaction of asking him why the
nurse was travelling with them.

Nick turned in the front passenger seat as she settled
herself and, with a mocking smile, informed her, 'In case

you're worried about who is looking after my father, his male nurse has returned from a weekend break. Sophia was just helping out for a couple of days.'

God! The man was a mind-reader, Abby thought resentfully, and did not bother to hide her disgust as she responded, 'Oh, really? How nice.' She felt a stirring of pity for the young girl—it was obvious she adored 'Nico', as she called him. He really was a ruthless swine without an ounce of shame in his body.

The journey passed remarkably quickly under the circumstances, Jonathan's chatter hiding any tension between the adults. The transfer to the company jet and the flight to Athens was accomplished without a hitch, but by the time they were standing on the pavement outside the airport hostilities were resumed with a vengeance.

Abby watched as Nick kissed the young girl on the cheek and murmured something to her, and she could not hold back her snort of disgust. Nick turned angrily towards Abby, but just at that moment a strikingly handsome young man dashed up and swept Sophia into his arms. The introduction was brief—it was Leo, the girl's fiancé—and the pair of them said goodbye and walked away hand in hand.

'I think you owe that girl an apology, my dear,' Nick drawled mockingly. 'You should be ashamed of your disgusting thoughts.'

The fact that he had read her mind yet again only made Abby more angry, and she retaliated sarcastically, 'Really? I don't think so. A little thing like a fiancé never stopped you before. I was engaged to Harry not so long ago, remember?'

'Hardly the same thing,' he sneered. 'Sophia is still a virgin. You, on the other hand, have been round the block a few times and are fair game——'

'You bastard! H——'

'Shut up and get in the car.'

It was then she noticed that a large, chauffeur-driven limousine had stopped at the kerbside.

'Are you and Daddy pretending to fight again?' Jonathan

piped up, his little hand pulling at her skirt.

Oh, no! How was it possible that this man could make her so angry that she forgot her own child? 'Yes, darling, something like that,' she said, shooting Nick a fulminating glance. It was all his fault. She helped Jonathan into the rear of the car and climbed in after him. Nick closed the door behind her and slid into the front passenger seat without speaking. She wondered where he was taking them, but did not ask. She tried to catch the conversation going on between Nick and the driver; she had a reasonably good understanding of Greek. It was one of the things she had tried to do to impress him and keep her marriage alive the first time, but it hadn't worked. Lost in her own thoughts, and with Jonathan asleep in the crook of her arm, she was shocked to realise they had passed Athens and were now wending their way up a hillside, but her mouth hung open in stunned amazement when the car eventually stopped.

It was her house . . . The house she had planned all those years ago, with such love and so many bright dreams, but they had all crumbled to dust at her feet as Nick had revealed his true nature.

She could not look at him as he opened the door and lifted Jonathan from her arms. How dared he bring her here? Her lovely eyes misted with tears, and angrily she brushed them away. She was being stupidly sentimental. Of course he would have kept the house. It was a good investment, a valuable bit of real estate.

Tall cypress trees, pointing to the sky like a circle of church spires, surrounded a gently sloping clearing, and in the centre nestled a long, low, two-storeyed house, built to fit the curve of the hill. She swallowed the lump forming in her throat. How well she remembered the design. The hours they had spent deciding on the exact length of the balcony, the perfect spot for the swimming-pool. The clear, simple lines were a joy to her artistic eye, and it was with mixed feelings of fear and anticipation that she followed Nick up to the entrance door, where a small, plump, grey-headed woman, her homely face wreathed in smiles, was waiting.

'Mr Kardis, and your lovely wife, welcome home. Oh, and isn't he an angel?' She chortled as Jonathan, waking up, demanded to be put down.

Abby's eyes widened in amazement; the voice sounded so incongruous in a villa in Greece. It was pure East End.

'Yes, you're right. Mary is a Londoner to her fingertips.' Putting an arm around the older woman, Nick hugged her briefly before adding, 'And my treasured housekeeper. Her husband Henry is half Greek and acts as my chauffeur.' Before she could respond to the introduction, Abby found her feet dangling in mid-air as Nick swept her up into his arms and carried her over the threshold, drawling, 'Welcome home, Abby darling.'

'What do you think you're doing?' she snapped furiously, the sound of Jonathan's and Mary's laughter ringing in her ears. 'Put me down.'

'It's traditional, darling, and so is this.' And to her chagrin he set her on her feet and covered her mouth with his own in a long, drugging kiss that left her breathless. Her face was as red as her hair as she stared at him, speechless, unable to think of a suitable rebuke. At least, not one she dared voice in front of other people. She had already upset her son once today by arguing with Nick, and she still felt guilty about it. Nick, his grey eyes teasing, knew damn well how she felt, and deliberately took advantage. Grasping her hand, he lifted it to his mouth and lightly kissed her fingers.

'Come on, I'll give you a tour of your dream home, Abby.' She wanted to pull her hand away, to scream that it was not her dream home any more, he had turned it into a nightmare years ago, but she couldn't, and as Mary led Jonathan away with the promise of milk and cookies she meekly allowed Nick to lead her into the lounge.

At first glance, she couldn't believe it. Her fingers tightened convulsively in his hard hand, and briefly she closed her eyes. She took a deep, calming breath and looked again. It was true. The satin damask sofa in mint and cream, the curtains, everything just as she had chosen them. How had he done it? That was easily answered—she had left samples of material and the correspondence with the interior designer all over the apartment, hoping to arouse Nick's interest, but it had not worked. So why? Why now?

Mutely she followed him from room to room, the formal dining-room, the family-room, the guest bedrooms; the colour schemes, the furnishings, were all exactly as she had chosen. She could not bear to look at him, but she could sense his eyes on her, watching, waiting for her reaction. Not by a flutter of an eyelash did she betray her tortured thoughts. Did he expect her congratulations? Was he really that unfeeling? Hmm, yes, he was . . . She felt as if she had been stabbed in the stomach, and someone were deliberately twisting the knife in the wound. How could he be so cruel? To bring her here, now, when their marriage was just a charade?

The house was perfect, exactly as she had envisaged it, with all her plans brought to fruition, and she felt like crying for her lost dreams. It was only when she walked into the room set aside for Jonathan that she managed to regain her control. Here everything was new. Long shelves full of all kinds of toys, a large frieze of Thomas the Tank Engine around the walls.

'This is nice, but I think you've overdone the toys a bit.' She spoke to a spot somewhere over Nick's left shoulder.

'So you do have a voice,' he drawled softly. 'I was beginning to wonder.'

'Yes, well, the rest is very nice,' she said blandly, proud of her ability to appear unaffected. 'Who did the interior for you?' she queried lightly. She was damned if she was going to give him the satisfaction of realising she recognised anything.

'I think you know very well, Abby, but just in case you have genuinely forgotten,' he intoned sardonically, 'maybe this will jog your memory.' And, tightening his grip on her hand, he led her into the master bedroom.

The king-size bed dominated one wall; the peach curtains were yet another of her choices. Another wall was one long run of mirrored wardrobes, Nick the sensualist's suggestion—actually he had suggested the ceiling, but she had laughingly refused. The memory only increased the pain she did not want to feel, but she did not have time to dwell on it as he hurried her along to the far end of the room. Reaching from floor to ceiling, a long mahogany screen slid back to reveal on a raised dais a huge cream circular whirlpool and jacuzzi, with ornate gold trimming, and above it a domed glass roof.

'Remember, Abby?' Nick's voice vibrated against her ear. She tried to pull away, but he would not let her, and, turning her into his arms, he forced her to face him by the simple expedient of wrapping her long hair around his wrist and pulling her head back. 'Did I tell you I love your hair long? And it's so useful,' he opined, and for a long moment he held her. She shivered as the heat of his hard-muscled body burnt into hers, the spicy male scent of him enveloping her.

'You do remember,' he taunted mockingly.

She forced herself to meet his eyes, and flinched at the angry desire he could not quite hide, but then something odd happened. As they stared at each other, the anger, the resentment faded. The years rolled back and they were sharing the same memory. Nick's eyes softened, his hard lips twitched and lifted at the corners in a reminiscent smile that Abby involuntarily responded to. She could not help it; a soft chuckle escaped her.

It had been in the old apartment. She had been in the bath, a very ordinary bath-tub, and Nick had stripped off and joined her. With his six feet plus, and with Abby being no midget herself, it had been a tight but interesting squeeze. Until Nick's long moan of shattering release had turned into a high-pitched yell as he'd almost broken his toe on the bath-tap. Afterwards, lying in bed together, they had planned the extravagant jacuzzi. He'd reckoned every home should have one erotic fantasy incorporated into it. They would lie in the bath bathed in moonlight, watching the stars and the rest . . .

'We had some great times, Abby . . .' he murmured throatily, lowering his head to hers. 'Shall we?'

She swayed closer, and his hands gently stroked her back, his hold gentle now. His lips brushed hers . . . She was tempted, oh, so tempted . . .

'You love it . . . You know you do,' he husked.

His words were like a douche of cold water. It, she thought bitterly. That was all anything was to Nick. Shocked back to reality, she pushed him away and ran from the room.

He caught her on the landing. 'Wait a minute. I haven't finished yet,' he declared with a frown.

'Well, I have. If you don't mind, I would like to go and find Jonathan.' She cursed the quaver in her voice, but could not control it. His total lack of any genuine feeling appalled her, more so than ever in this house that had once seemed to promise so much.

'I'm not going to drag you into the bedroom, Abby,' he mocked her obvious agitation, 'but there is another room I want to show you.'

Warily she followed him through a door that should have led on to the flat roof of the garage, but instead she found it was a studio. It was incredible; she couldn't believe it. She looked all around her in a daze, and then wandered from end to end—everything she could possibly want was here: water-colours, oils, pastels, sable brushes, a large easel, and a smaller one for outdoors, an assortment of canvases every shape and size, and the room itself was perfect, the whole of the north wall one huge plate-glass window.

'Do you like it? I hope I haven't forgotten anything, but it was all done in a bit of a rush this last month. So is it OK?' He sounded so unsure, so hesitant, that she could only stare at him.

CHAPTER EIGHT

'OK?' SHE breathed, looking around in awe. A dream studio. OK didn't begin to describe it. 'It's fabulous—the light, everything is—is . . .' Words failed her and she looked up at him in puzzled wonder.

'Thank God! I got something right for you,' he said, with such heartfelt relief that she could almost believe he meant it. A broad grin slashed across his handsome face, and for the first time since their remarriage she forgot her angry resentment at his treatment of her and a matching smile curved her own full lips.

'I don't know why you did it, Nick!' she exclaimed, flinging her arms wide to encompass the whole room. 'But I love it! Thank you.'

Laughing at her enthusiasm, he caught her outstretched hand. 'Come and sit down and I'll tell you,' he commanded, and, leading her to a long leather seating unit placed against one wall, he sat down, pulling her down beside him. Abby made no resistance, her mind already focused on her first painting, an oil perhaps, of the house itself, or maybe she would try a portrait . . .

'I know you think of me as a ruthless, arrogant swine, who will do anything to get what I want, and I freely admit I am in some ways——' He stopped. 'Abby, are you listening?'

'What? Oh, yes,' she responded, only half aware of what he was saying, but gradually as he continued her brief sense of euphoria faded away.

'The first time I walked into your gallery, I was stunned to see that a couple of the paintings were your own. I had lived with you for over a year, and never known you were an artist. I thought of you as my young, beautiful possession, to be indulged and protected. Looking back, I can see I didn't really know you at all. You're a much

stronger woman than I ever gave you credit for.' All the time
he spoke his strong hand cradled Abby's.

What was he up to now? she wondered cynically,
fighting down the flush of heat that his thumb, idly
stroking her palm, was arousing. Warning bells rang in
her head. A humble, complimentary Nick was an
unknown quantity, and much more dangerous to her
peace of mind.

'That is all very flattering, Nick, but you still haven't told
me—why the studio?' she prompted stiffly. He had gone to
an awful lot of trouble when she only intended staying a
few short months. Didn't she . . .?

'I'm coming to that,' he responded softly, tightening his
hold on her hand as she made to pull free. 'In the past I was
wrong, you were strong enough to know the truth, and I
should have told you, but at least I can learn by my
mistakes.'

Abby stiffened at his words. She guessed what he meant.
Strong was not the word, but *stoic*—able to put up with his
mistresses and run a home and family. She shot a sidelong
glance at his arrogant features. Thank God she had got
over him, because he would certainly never change. Why
the thought saddened her she did not question, the
realisation that it did was more than she wanted to
acknowledge . . .

'When I met you again in September, Abby,' Nick
continued, self-derision evident in his tone, 'it was brought
home to me, very succinctly, that, unlike most women of
my acquaintance, you don't have an avaricious bone in your
body. Jewellery, money mean very little to you. You
relished telling me how you had given away the divorce
settlement,' he opined wryly.

Her delicate brows drew together in a worried frown. She
might have guessed he would get back to the money some
day.

'Don't look so worried, sweetheart,' he drawled, his grey
eyes twinkling down on to her wary green ones. 'I'm
delighted at the way you disposed of it. It was much
preferable to the use I had envisaged. I assure you.'

Curiosity got the better of her, and she could not resist asking, 'What exactly did you think I had done with the money?'

'Harkness,' he muttered in response, his grey eyes narrowing intently on her lovely face, almost as though he was seeking reassurance.

She stared at him in amazement. 'Ian Harkness?' she queried.

'Why not? He was a struggling artist years ago, he needed someone to back him, and you did leave Greece with him.'

When the import of his words sunk in, Abby could not restrain her laughter. Ian belonged to a very wealthy family, and if he never sold a painting in his life he would not starve. 'You mean he was my gigolo?' She chuckled. 'That's not very flattering, I have never needed to pay a man yet,' she could not resist teasing, then sobered instantly at the tight-lipped anger in his face. 'Anyway, it was coincidence our being on the same plane for England.' She did not know why she was bothering to tell Nick, he certainly did not deserve any explanations from her, but still she carried on. 'It was another two years before I saw Ian again, and then it was only by accident.' Withdrawing her hand from his, she waited.

'Really . . .? Well, that's not important now,' he dismissed. 'What I'm trying to say is, this studio is your wedding present in lieu of the more conventional diamond necklace, and——' he grinned a wide, boyish smile that inexplicably made her heart ache '——it does have one great advantage: you can't throw it in my face.'

She did not return his smile. A wedding present, he'd said, and yet he must have had the builder working on the studio long before he had asked her—no, not asked, coerced her into marrying him. How typically arrogant, and worse, it reaffirmed Melanie's story. The anger she wanted to feel didn't surface; instead she was prey to more ambivalent emotions, one of which was regret, but why it should be so she did not understand, or perhaps did not want to . . .

As though reading her mind, Nick caught her chin in one strong hand and forced her to face him. 'I know what you are thinking, and you are right. I did plan the studio straight after seeing you and Jonathan in St Ives. I admit I'm ruthless when it is something I really want——'

'And of course you always get what you want,' she cut in angrily, in an effort to quell her unease. For once she would have preferred the diamonds. Jewellery could be left without a qualm when they parted, but there was something seductively permanent about the studio, and the thought frightened her.

'Not always, but I try,' he said hardly, his grey eyes searching her face as though expecting a response.

Belatedly Abby remembered her innate good manners. 'I see. Well, thank you very much, it is a lovely room,' she accepted his present with as much grace as she could muster.

'My pleasure,' Nick drawled. 'And, talking about pleasure, the last two days, we have either made love——'

Abby arched one brow speakingly—that wasn't what she would have called it.

'All right,' his firm lips quirked in an ironic smile, 'we have either had sex . . . or fought. The first in private, the second in public. It is not good for Jonathan to see us constantly at each other's throat. Now we are in our own home I intend to ensure we live like any other normal family, and, contrary to what you may think, or imagine, I want you and Jonathan to be happy here—hence the studio.'

For the space of a heartbeat, Abby almost believed it was genuine affection that shone in his smoky grey eyes. Knocking his hand from her chin abruptly, she jumped up and walked across the room to stare mistily out of the huge window. He was getting to her again. She could not deny it, and that way lay madness. She breathed deeply, and tensed as she sensed him move to stand directly behind her. His long arms folded around her waist and pulled her back against him. She could feel the sudden electric tension in the atmosphere. A shiver of sensual awareness rippled down her spine, and the temptation to lean back into his hard·body, to let his vibrant, masculine sexuality overwhelm her, was almost impossible to resist.

'Truce, Abby,' he murmured huskily, bending his head to nuzzle her throat with soft, warm lips.

Truce, she thought bleakly. The dictionary definition was a respite, a temporary peace or interruption of war by agreement. Perhaps she could live with Nick on those terms, but her woman's intuition told her that was not his true intention. For a moment, held in his arms, his musky male scent enveloping her, she was sorely tempted, but she knew that if she accepted the reality would be her complete surrender. Once again she would be the little wife at home and in his bed, a convenience for as long as it suited him, and she had too much self-respect for that. No way, she silently vowed.

It took every inch of will power she possessed to turn in his arms and push him away. 'A truce is not necessary,' she managed to say casually.' Though I do take your point in regard to Jonathan, but we are both mature adults, and I'm sure with a little effort we can successfully hide our differences from him.' She was proud of her self-control as she made to walk past him, but it was stretched to the limit when his large hand fastened around her wrist like a manacle. She looked up into his smoky grey eyes, turbulent with some emotion. Was it pain that she glimpsed? No, frustrated anger more like, because she had denied him an easy victory.

'You, a mature adult, Abby?' he derided. 'I'm beginning to——' Whatever scathing comment he was about to make was never voiced as Jonathan erupted into the studio.

'Mary said lunch is ready, and will you hurry up? I'm hungry.'

Abby turned smiling eyes on to her son, 'All right, darling, let's eat, and maybe afterwards we can explore the garden, hmm?' She desperately needed some fresh air, to get away from Nick's disturbing presence, but it didn't

quite work out as she had planned. After lunch Nick insisted
on accompanying them on a tour of the grounds.

They walked across the gently sloping lawn, with
Jonathan happily skipping along between them. Abby
breathed deeply of the fresh mountain air and gradually
the tension of the past two days faded away. Abby
looked around her, delighted. The house and garden
were everything she had ever hoped they would be. She
glanced at Nick. The breeze lifted a lock of dark hair
across his brow, and she looked away, disturbed by an
almost irresistible urge to smooth it back. The
treacherous thought assailed her that they looked like a
normal, happy family unit, but somehow she did not
seem to mind.

They stopped to admire the huge rock-pool, the
centre-point of the garden, naturally landscaped and
surrounded by a mass of late-blooming flowers of red and
gentian blue, and with a simple dolphin fountain in the
middle. Nick crouched on his haunches to explain the finer
mechanics of how the fountain worked to Jonathan, and the
child listened with all the determination of a small boy
intent on discovering everything he could from his new
daddy.

The two heads so close together, black hair gleaming in
the autumnal sun, were so alike that it brought a lump to
Abby's throat. She swallowed hard and walked on towards
the circle of trees. Jonathan was going to miss Nick when
the inevitable parting came, and there was no way she could
protect him from the hurt. Was there?

'Mummy, there are not as many pointy trees here as there
were at the house yesterday. It had hundreds at the
back.'

Nick came up behind them and chuckled. 'The reason is
quite simple, son. At your grandfather's house all the fir
trees belong to Aunty Catherine,' he told him with a
grin.

'But why, Daddy?'

'Well, when a girl is born it is the custom to plant as many
cypress trees as the parents can afford. When the girl grows

up and is married the trees are her dowry.'

'What is a do . . . dowry?' Jonathan asked, intrigued by the new word.

Abby smiled wryly, wondering how Nick would explain a typically Greek chauvinistic custom.

'It is a gift from the bride to her husband. You are old enough to understand that a woman brings the warmth into a man's life. At your age it is your mummy; when you are as old as I am it should be your wife. The trees are symbolic, but also very practical. Enough, and a woman can keep the fire burning a lifetime for her husband.' Nick's gaze clashed with Abby's over the top of Jonathan's head. 'Isn't that so, Abby?' he demanded hardly, and she flushed at the smouldering question in his silver eyes that had mothing to do with trees.

'Did you give daddy any trees?' Jonathan piped up, breaking the thread of sexual tension between his parents with his question. A worried frown creased his little brow as he waited for an answer.

'No, darling, in England we don't do that,' she hastily reassured him, and watched, intrigued, as he quite seriously looked up at the tall trees for a long time. She could almost see his fertile brain ticking over, then finally he turned to Nick, a broad smile replacing his worried frown.

'I know. We are all electric in my house, so Mummy must have given you electric.'

Nick, his dark head thrown back, roared with laughter, his white teeth gleaming in the tanned perfection of his handsome face.

'Jonathan, my boy,' he spluttered, 'your logic is unbeatable. You're right, so very right. Your mother creates electricity for me all the time.' And it was true . . .

Abby met his dancing eyes, and broke up . . . Nick put his arm around her shaking shoulders, and for the first time in years their shared laughter echoed joyously in the clear air.

Abby threw the paintbrush down in disgust, and with a brief derogatory glance at the canvas in front of her she walked

out of the studio. It had become her sanctuary over the past
five weeks, but today not even her painting could calm her
troubled thoughts. She wandered into the master bedroom,
and wearily sank down on the edge of the wide bed, her
shoulders slumped in an attitude of total dejection.

Nick had taken over her life with an implacable
determination she could not oppose. He had enrolled
Jonathan at a nearby nursery school, true, and he had asked
her opinion, but only because he had known she would
agree. Jonathan returned at lunchtime, and by the time
they'd eaten and he'd had his nap she barely had a couple
of hours alone with her son before Nick arrived home.

At first it had hurt to see Jonathan run straight to his
father as soon as he walked in the door, but gradually
she had come to accept it, as she was forced to concede
that Nick was a wonderful father. He knew exactly how
to talk to Jonathan and what amused him. Unfortunately
the growing relationship between father and son only
made Abby feel more threatened. Her own relationship
with Nick was nowhere near as simple to understand.

More and more often of late, she found herself
questioning her own emotions. Nick confused and
confounded her at every turn. She bitterly resented the way
he made her feel, and Nick, damn him, knew it . . . He
refused to fight with her, deflecting all her insulting
remarks and barbed comments with cool mockery or,
worse, a patient indulgence, as though she were a small,
fractious child. It made her blood boil.

Much to her amazement, Nick returned from the office
on the dot of six every night. If he had other women, she
could not imagine where he got the time or energy from!
They spent a surprisingly companionable happy hour or
two with Jonathan before putting him to bed, and then they
dressed for dinner.

It was afterwards that Abby feared most. Nick was an
aggressively masculine man, with a kind of raw virility that
was almost impossible to resist, and once they were alone
he made no attempt to hide his desire for her. Usually by
the time they were halfway through their after-dinner drink

the air crackled with sexual tension. Abby either goaded him until he stalked off, tight-lipped, to his study, or they went straight to bed. It didn't matter which, she acknowledged wryly; the end result was always the same. It was the early hours of the morning before they slept.

Only once had she tried to deny him. The first night in their 'dream home' she had deliberately gone to the small guest-room, determined she was not going to give in quietly to him. She had been almost asleep when he had walked in. In the dim moonlight he had towered over her, large and formidable, his only clothing a dark, silk, thigh-length robe. She had expected him to be furious, but he amazed her. He didn't speak, just shrugged off his robe, threw back the covers and slid into the narrow bed beside her.

'What do you think you're doing?' she'd cried, intensely aware of his hard, naked body pressed tightly against her own. 'You have a perfectly good bed along the hall,' she'd muttered.

'I know, Abby darling, but if my wife prefers to sleep in a cosy narrow bed, who am I to argue?' he had drawled mockingly.

'Don't be ridiculous,' she'd snapped, almost falling out of the bed in her haste to get away from him.

'I am not being ridiculous, but I'm not so sure about you, sweetheart,' Nick had said cynically. 'I spent an hour the other morning, while you were still asleep, explaining to our son why his parents shared a bed. He was somewhat jealous when he found you sleeping with me, and I had to put him straight. I have no intention of reversing the conversation tomorrow morning.'

'I didn't know that,' Abby had murmured.

'It's your decision, Abby—here, or the master bedroom, but certainly with me,' Nick had declared hardly.

Meekly she'd agreed, and Nick had swung her up in his strong arms and carried her into the master bedroom. She could not do much else; he was right and she knew it. Later that night she had awakened to Nick's hand gently caressing her breast. He had proceeded to make love to her with a controlled patience that almost drove her out of her mind.

Abby shuddered, her body flushing with heat at the memory. She jumped off the bed. She didn't want to think about his lovemaking. Didn't want to admit he was a wonderful lover. Ever since that night he had treated her with a mixture of tenderness and passion that she was humiliatingly aware she could not resist. Sometimes he would lie for hours examining, admiring every inch of her naked body with a connoisseur's appreciation of a beautiful rare object, and she was helpless to stop him, lost in the sensual delight his touch aroused in her.

Restless and on edge, Abby walked downstairs to the kitchen. A note on the refrigerator door told her Mary had gone shopping. She frowned and wandered out to the family-room, where she tiredly collapsed into an overstuffed armchair.

Abby curled her feet up under her in the big chair, and gazed sightlessly out of the window. The last few weeks had not been bad. She loved the house and garden, and her studio was a constant source of delight, but today she could have used a friend to confide in. She called Iris twice a week, but it was not the same any more. So much had happened, Cornwall seemed a lifetime away, and it was unsettling to realise Iris ran the gallery as well as, if not better than, she had.

It was painful to have to admit, but her real problem was in sustaining her long-held hatred of Nick. It was becoming harder and harder to actively dislike a man who gave her so much pleasure, and not just in the sexual sense. Nick had a keen mind, and on occasions they talked for hours on a wide variety of subjects, from music to politics and art. To Abby's surprise she found herself agreeing with his views more often than not. Then there had been the episode with the clothes.

Nick had taken her into Athens and insisted on buying her a whole new wardrobe. She had tried to refuse, saying she preferred her own casual look. Nick had silenced her objection by agreeing with her; he'd laughed and told her he loved her 'derrière' in blue jeans—it was an instant turn-on—but that the lavish gowns were for the formal occasions she would have to attend with him as the holiday season approached.

Last night had been the first such occasion, and Abby was still reeling from the shock. The dinner had been held at a private club and hosted by a business acquaintance of Nick's. They'd arrived and were shown to their seats, when to Abby's horror she had discovered they were sharing a table with Dolores Stakis, with a much younger man in tow. Abby had sat all night, sick to her stomach and barely saying a word, while Nick had joked and laughed with their companions. To make matters worse, in any other circumstances she would have thought Dolores a nice lady. Her congratulations on their remarriage had sounded perfectly genuine. Unfortunately, by the end of the night, Abby had been so eaten up by jealousy that she had made a totally unwarranted remark to Dolores. She could hear it in her head even now, twelve hours later, and still could not believe she had said it. 'I see that, like a lot of older actresses these days, you prefer young men.'

Nick had been furious. He had apologised to Dolores and bundled Abby out and into the car. He had not spoken one word until they were home and in bed; then he had turned on her.

His grey eyes had been as cold and as bleak as the Arctic ocean. 'I warned you once before about insulting my family and friends, and this is the last time. Don't you ever dare do that again, or I will turn you over my knee and give you the good hiding you deserve.'

Abby had cringed at the contemptuous expression on his handsome face, and hadn't doubted him for a minute.

'I once thought I loved a delightful young girl, and I honestly believed you had matured into a strong, beautiful woman, but now I am beginning to wonder. You're a bitch, a first-class bitch.' And, turning his back on her, he had gone to sleeep. Abby had not been so lucky; she had listened to the deep, even sound of his breathing, tears pricking the back of her lids; she had gritted her teeth to prevent them spilling over. His words had hurt her deeply and she had had no defence against them.

Now, in the clear light of day, she raged silently inside at Nick. It was all his fault—he obviously thought nothing of dining out with his wife and ex-mistress. Why should that worry me? she thought bitterly, but she knew ...

Her own innate honesty forced her to admit that somewhere along the line Nick had breached her defences. She had thought, sex—why not? She could handle the physical attraction between them—after all, he was a devastatingly attractive man. But she had not realised how strong the attraction would grow. She took a long, hard look at herself and did not like what she saw. Jealousy was an unenviable emotion, and her remark last night had been unpardonable. Perhaps it was time she stopped sniping at Nick and took him at his face-value, instead of always looking for ulterior motives behind his every action. At least it was worth a try ... She wanted his good opinion. Why, Abby was not quite ready to face ...

Tomorrow they were going to Corfu, as they had done every weekend. She never thought she would have lived to see the day when the prospect of visiting Nick's father would give her pleasure, but it did. At the villa, with a house full of children, Nick was much more easy going. Perhaps it was relief at seeing his father, or maybe his reason was more cynical—a determination to keep his family in the dark about the true state of his marriage.

Whatever the reason, Abby did not care. She was just grateful for the respite from the ever-present tension between them in their own house. She could no more resist Nick's lazy, indulgent charm now than she had been able to five years ago, and she didn't question her own motive for going along with him. She didn't dare to ...

A reminiscent smile curved her mouth. Last weekend they had taken all but the youngest child on a picnic. Nick had organised the expedition. They had walked around the famous Kalami Bay, but he had refused to allow them to stop there, leading them instead up a steep gravel path and through a forest of trees, until they had reached a delightful little clearing. A clear stream gurgled through the centre, and a huge eucalyptus tree shaded a small natural pool of crystal-clear water.

After gorging themselves on chicken, cheese, crispy bread rolls, salad and potato chips, Nick had declared he was going to teach everyone to fish, armed with a stick and a piece of string, his version of a fishing-rod. A hilarious hour had ensued, with much screaming and laughter. If there had ever been any fish in the pool in the first place, which Abby seriously doubted, the noise they made must have long since chased them away. Finally they had reluctantly turned to pack up the picnic and go home, only to see a mangy old goat gobbling the last of it.

The children had yelled and flung their arms about in an effort to scare it off. Nick, perfectly straight-faced, had looked at Abby and said, 'I do believe it is the same animal. I am glad to see its taste has improved with age.'

'I think you're right,' she had agreed, deadpan, but she had not been able to prevent her lips twitching as she'd recalled his tattered jeans, and they had both burst out laughing. When their mirth had subsided, Nick had slanted her a brief, wry smile, oddly poignant.

'We always did share the same sense of humour.' Taking her small hand in his, he had added, 'And so much more.'

She had not argued with him, and hand in hand they had returned to the villa.

'Abby, Abby, where are you?' a deep voice echoed through the silent house, and Abby jumped out of the chair, every nerve jangling. What was Nick back for? It was barely noon.

'In here,' she called huskily, uneasily aware that she had not spoken to Nick since his angry words the previous evening. Perhaps he regretted them, the pleasing thought flashed into her mind, and that was why he was home early. But she was quickly disillusioned as he strode into the room. Abby looked up at his face and the expression in his steel-grey eyes was as remote and cold as Siberia.

Afterwards she only had a vague recollection of the

events of that day. Collecting Jonathan from nursery, a silent, grim-faced Nick on the flight to Corfu. Then Catherine's husband greeting them on the steps of the villa with the news. They were just too late; the old man had died half an hour ago. Her own softly voiced sympathy—'I'm sorry, Nick'—and his sardonic reply. 'Are you?'

She had cringed beneath his contemptuous expression, and, feeling inexplicably guilty, had spent the rest of the day looking after the children.

When they were in bed, she ate dinner with Theo as her only companion. Where Nick was, she had no idea . . . Later, lying in their huge bed, alone—where Nick was sleeping she did not know—she was unable to sleep, and instead tried to rationalise her own emotions. She was sorry about her father-in-law, but it had been expected, though not quite so quickly. She should be relieved; Nick would now gain absolute control of the company, and she . . . she could be back in St Ives by next week. There was nothing to stop her, and it was where she wanted to be. Wasn't it? So why was she crying? The tears ran freely down her cheeks, and, rolling over on to her stomach, she buried her head in the pillow in a futile attempt to stifle the rending sobs she could not control. She told herself she had got what she wanted, but the ache, the bone-deep loneliness in her heart, she could not explain away so easily.

She tossed and turned for hours, and it was just before the dawn that she finally admitted to herself that she missed Nick's hard-muscled body beside her, the touch of his hands, they thrusting power of his lovemaking that left her satiated and fulfilled. It wasn't love. It couldn't be. His earlier betrayal had cured her of that emotion, but neither was it just sex, as she had so foolishly tried to convince herself. She imagined this was how a junkie must feel going cold-turkey, hating the drug, knowing it was bad, but desperate for a fix . . . Sighing, her tears subdued, she turned over to Nick's side of the bed. Well, she had the rest of her life to get over the addiction, she told herself, but the thought did nothing to assuage the aching need in her body or her overheated flesh. She went to sleep at last from sheer exhaustion.

The next morning, Abby, pale but composed, supervised the children's breakfast. So far they had reacted to their grandfather's death very well, perhaps because they were too young to appreciate the finality of death. They still chattered and laughed, but a little less exuberantly then usual. The only one who caused Abby any problem was the youngest girl, at barely two, who was obviously missing her mummy's attention. Abby had just tied the baby's bib for the third time when Nick walked into the breakfast-room.

She glanced up. His tanned, perfectly carved features were set in a cold mask. His tall, lean body was clad in a black three-piece suit, tailored to perfection to emphasise the width of his shoulders and the lean, masculine elegance of his hips and thighs. She could not control the nervous leaping of her pulse as her eyes met his, betraying how much she had missed him.

'Nick, I wondered whe——' Unthinkingly she burst into speech, only to be cut off abruptly.

'My God, woman, can't you wait until the poor devil is in his grave before wondering when you can leave?' She recoiled beneath the icy anger in his tone. 'I have no intention of discussing our private affairs now. Catherine, understandably, is distraught. All I want from you is your assurance that you will take care of the children until after the funeral tomorrow. They are too young to attend.'

'Yes, yes, of course,' she responded immediately.

'Thank you ... I guessed you wouldn't mind missing the funeral,' he opined sarcastically, and, turning on his heel, walked out.

'Mummy, is Daddy angry?'

She turned dazed eyes to her son. 'No, he's not angry, darling, just upset,' she soothed, glad Nick had misconstrued her words. She had almost asked him where he'd spent the night, and made a complete fool of herself.

It was ten in the evening. Jonathan was fast asleep next door, but Abby did not feel in the least like going to bed.

The house that had been full of sombrely dressed visitors all day was now silent and strangely oppressive. Quickly slipping out of the formal wool dress she had worn for dinner, she pulled on a favourite old navy velour jogging-suit, and, slipping her feet into a pair of scruffy trainers, she quietly made her way downstairs and out into the garden. She had to get away from the cloying atmosphere of the house, or scream . . .

She drew a deep, refreshing breath of the cool night air and expelled it in a sigh. A slight breeze blew in off the Ionian sea, and she shivered as she gazed up at a billion twinkling stars in the vast, dark canopy of the heavens.

She ran down the avenue of trees, starkly outlined by the ghostly light of a clear crescent moon, to the small gate that led to the cove. Breathless for a moment, she leant on the top spar, drinking in the beauty of the night, but to her surprise, the gate swung open. That's odd, she thought. Nick always insisted it was locked; only a couple of weeks ago he had flatly refused to allow the children down on to the beach, insisting it was much too dangerous.

With hesitant steps she carefully descended the rocky path. She loved the sea, and tonight she felt particularly homesick for St Ives. There the beach met the road and daily she had walked or run along it. She stopped, as her eyes caught a flash of white, barely twenty feet away. As she watched the shadow took shape and she recognised Nick. He was leaning against a jagged rock, his dark head bowed, his shoulders shaking. A stab of pain squeezed her heart. Never in her life had she seen any man look so desolate . . .

Like a puppet pulled by an invisible string, she walked towards him. It hurt her to see such a proud man cry. 'Nick! she didn't realise she had said his name out loud. His head jerked up and for a second she glimpsed a look of such anguish, such suffering in his eyes that her own problems were forgotten and she instinctively wanted to comfort him.

'Come to gloat?' he queried sarcastically, but she heard

the tremor in his voice that he could not quite disguise.

'No, Nick.' She stopped a foot away from him, compassion stirring within her, filling her with a tenderness she'd never expected to feel again for this hard, ruthless man. 'I thought you might like a friend, someone to talk to.'

'And are you my friend, Abby?' he asked musingly, almost as though he was talking to himself. 'I sometimes wonder if friendship exists any more.'

He sounded so remote, so lonely that Abby's throat ached suddenly and she blinked to rid her eyes of tears.

'Oh, Nick,' she murmured. Whatever their differences, she hated to see him like this.

'Oh, Abby,' he mocked, straightening up. 'Let me guess what you want to talk about. When you can leave, hmm?'

She knew intuitively that this was not the time to discuss her future, and, determined not to let him know how much his callous opinion of her hurt. She responded quietly, 'No, tonight I want to forget everything and just appreciate the beauty of the surroundings. This is an exquisite bay. Why does no one use it?'

'Why? Because I forbid it,' he said with some of his old arrogance, and then, in a complete about-turn, his voice lowered wearily. 'Ah, what's the use? You think I am every kind of villain; you might as well know I'm also a coward.'

She looked up at him in surprise, and shivered at the black emptiness she saw in his eyes. Seeing her reaction, he reached out and pulled her into his arms. One strong hand gently rubbed her back while the other eased her hips between his splayed legs. 'You're cold,' he murmured, but there was nothing sensual about his embrace.

'No. But what about you?' she asked softly. He had shed his jacket somewhere, and a white silk dress-shirt was no protection against the cool night air.

'I never feel the cold, but, contrary to what you think, I do have feelings, I am human, with all the human weaknesses.'

'You, weak? Never,' she tried to tease, but he ignored her comment or perhaps didn't hear it. Locked in his arms, felling oddly protected by his hard masculine body instead of feeling threatened, she listened to him continue.

'I have never been on this beach for almost twenty years. I've hated it that long.'

Abby squashed the question that leapt to her tongue; she had an idea she was finally going to get an insight into her husband's character, and she didn't want to stop him.

'You were right about this house.' He gave her a ghost of a smile. 'It has never been a happy place. My grandfather built it in the twenties. He made a fortune in America, married a New York girl and brought her back here. She hated it.'

So that's where the grey eyes came from, Abby realised; he had never mentioned his grandparents before.

'You can't really blame her; in those days there were only a few people living here. She left when my father was five and he never forgave her. My grandfather was the opposite; he worshipped her till the day he died. She had three more husbands and between each one, like a fool, he would take her back. My father reckoned it taught him a valuable lesson, and when he married he chose a local Greek peasant girl. One who knew what was expected of her. Unfortunately for my mother, she fell in love with him. She ignored his numerous mistresses like a good Greek wife, but he went too far in the end and actually brought his lady-friend here. My mother left them in the house, walked down here and into the sea. I found her body on the beach a day later. I was nineteen at the time, and even now my father is dead I still can't forgive him.'

'Oh, Nick, how terrible for you,' she murmured, horrified at the thought of a young Nick having to deal with such a situation.

He hugged her tightly. 'I always knew you had a soft centre,' he mocked softly, before continuing, 'It wasn't just my mother. A few months later my grandfather died;

he had a heart attack while swimming here. But the final straw was my friend Spiros. We had been pals all our lives, we went everywhere together, and at twenty I was best man at his wedding to his very pregnant bride. The day his daughter was born we had a few drinks and went out for a sail. It was our favourite sport. A storm blew up, and he was knocked overboard.' Abby could sense the tension in him, the effort it was taking just to get the words out, and her heart went out to him. 'I couldn't save him. I tried . . . God, how I tried. We had lost the main mast, the auxiliary engine flooded, and it was eighteen hours before I was picked up. I've never put a foot in the sea or sailed on it since. So now you know. I'm a coward. I should have faced up to my fears long ago.'

Abby could not find words to express her horror at his story; instead she put her slender arms around his waist and hugged him as she would a child, trying to absorb some of his pain.

Gently he lifted her chin with one long finger. 'No mocking comment, Abby?' he asked wryly, his grey eyes intent upon her pale face. She returned his scrutiny and for an unguarded moment he allowed her to see into his soul; the hidden sadness, the vulnerable man, open to fear and pain, the same as anyone else. And then it hit her . . .

She closed her eyes as the shock shuddered through her body. God in heaven, why? her mind screamed as in a flash of blinding clarity she was forced to recognise what she had refused to acknowledge for weeks. No, years. She loved this man. Had always loved him, and always would. It didn't seem to matter what he did, how he humiliated her; seeing him unsure and hurting had revealed what she should have known all along. She loved him, and his pain was hers. She opened her eyes to find him smiling down at her with tender concern.

'Come on, Abby, I'll take you home. I can feel you shivering. I must be mad, keeping you here listening to my phobias.' And with his arm around her shoulders he led her over the sand to the cliff path. She was aware of his thigh

brushing hers, the warmth of his hand on her shoulder as
they walked, but, as for the rest, he could have been taking
her anywhere. Her mind was in a state of shock. She had
hated him for so long, antagonised him at every
opportunity, but now she saw her hatred for what it was; a
barrier to hide behind. Her deepest feminine instincts had
warned her he was a threat to the peaceful life she enjoyed
in Cornwall, so she had used a sharp tongue and snide
remarks to protect herself. Only she had failed. Seeing Nick
in his one and only moment of weakness had burst the
self-deluding bubble she had floated around in for weeks,
leaving her emotions raw and exposed. They were back in
the house before she'd recovered her wits enough to query
his story. Wait a minute . . . he had left her to go on a cruise
with Dolores. As soon as the thought entered her head she
blurted it out.

'No, I didn't.' He stopped halfway up the grand staircase,
and with a shame-faced smile he admitted, 'After I left the
apartment I booked into the Hilton. How else do you think
I knew you were on the same plane as Harkness? I checked
up on you the next day.'

She knew he was telling the truth, and sadly she realised
it didn't make much difference. The other woman more
than likely stayed at the hotel with him. Still, it amazed her
that she had never noticed before his fear of the sea.
Looking back, she could see it had been obvious. On their
honeymoon, at a string of different hotels, they had never
gone further than the swimming-pools. And there was his
adamant refusal to allow the children on to the beach here,
and at Kalami. She remembered the Sunday he had arrived
in St Ives and he had gone white when she'd told him
Jonathan was out sailing. All these things made perfect
sense now, but what she could not understand was why he
had been down on the beach this evening.

'Why, tonight, did you go on the beach? she asked
curiously. Nick opened the bedroom door and, with a hand
on her back, ushered her in before replying.

'Perhaps because, with the death of my father, I am now
the oldest member of my family. It's a very sobering

thought. Maybe trying to conquer my irrational fear of the sea is my way of proving I'm worthy of being head of the family, hmm?' He turned to face her, his fingers deftly unfastening his shirt and shrugging it off. 'Isn't that what a psychiatrist would say?' he queried, offering her the glimmer of a smile.

When she did not respond he took a step towards her and, cupping her face in his palms, he tilted her head up to his. Her heart began to hammer against her ribs and she murmured, 'Probably.' With her new-found knowledge of her love still at the forefront of her mind, she was terrified of betraying herself. His near-naked body, the familiar male scent of him, were having a disastrous effect upon her senses. She ached to feel the satin smoothness of his skin against hers.

Now she knew why she had missed him so desperately last night, and a nervous tremor raced through her. He must never find out. He had trampled on her pride, destroyed her self-respect once, and she'd have to be a prize fool to let him do it a second time. He lowered his head and his lips brushed lightly across her mouth, back and forth in a pleading kiss that awakened a thousand little nerve-ends to the rapture of his touch.

Her fears faded, and there was only Nick and herself, and the racing of her traitorous pulse.

'Abby. Help me. I need you . . . I need you so badly.' He groaned the words against her mouth.

He needed her, and that was enough. With a sigh she swayed into his arms, her small hands slid around his neck and urged his mouth back to hers. For tonight, at least, she was going to live solely for the moment. . .

He swung her up in his arms and carried her to the bed. In seconds they were both naked; strong hands feverishly caressed her shoulders, her breasts, as Nick's lips parted hers in a wild, drugging kiss. She held his head to hers, exulting in the silky, crisp feel of his hair around her fingers. Her body arched sensuously into his and he groaned against her mouth. She felt the hardness of desire in his thighs, and moaned with pleasure as his mouth captured her breast, tugging erotically on the rigid nipple, first one then the other. Their night apart could have been a hundred, their need for each other was so urgent. Their bodies joined in a primitive, desperate passion that immediately erupted in an explosive crescendo. She heard Nick call her name and then the full weight of his magnificent body slumped down on her, and she knew they had reached the peak of ecstasy together. He buried his head in her shoulder, his lips hot against her throat.

'God! Abby,' he rasped. 'No other woman in the world can make me feel the way you do.'

At that moment she believed him, and almost admitted she had never known another man, but unbidden came a cynical little thought: but he's not averse to trying to find a woman who might. So instead she compromised and murmured softly, 'I know. I feel the same,' and, running her slender hands over his broad shoulders and down his back, gently tracing every muscle and sinew, she longed to tell him she loved him, but knew, sadly, that she probably never would.

Nick rolled off her, and pulled her tenderly into the warmth of his side. 'Oh, Abby, I needed that!' he drawled throatily. 'You can't imagine how much,' he sighed.

She levered herself up on one elbow and looked down at his darkly flushed face. She lifted a finger and gently traced the furrow between his dark brows, the elegant line of his nose, and the outline of his sensuous mouth. Her heart full of love for him, she murmured, 'You look tired.'

His strong hands reached up and threaded through her tangled mane of hair. Bringing her head down to his, he kissed her long and thoroughly. 'Never too tired for you, witch,' he growled huskily.

She lay spread-eagled over his broad frame, her breasts pressed lightly against the curling hair of his muscular chest. She could feel the stirrings of renewed desire in his taut thighs, and she chuckled. 'You were last night.'

Nick did not share her amusement; instead he regarded her with an oddly serious expression. 'Abby, I know I shattered your trust in me once, and I've bitterly regretted it every second since, but we are together again, and as my wife you are entitled to know everything I do. So why don't you ask me where I was last night? I can tell you're dying to know.'

Colour suffused her face and her lips quirked in a wry smile. 'Am I so easy to read?' she asked.

'No, not at all,' he dismissed incredulously. 'I only wish you were. It's only the rare times you allow me to get close to you that I have the slightest inkling of how your mind works. But, to satisfy your curiosity, I spent the night in the study.' His arms tightened around her as he added wickedly, 'And not in bed with Marta, as you probably imagined.'

Marta!' she exclaimed, her green eyes lit with laughter. 'How could you insult the poor woman?' A vivid picture of the elderly housekeeper and Nick together teased her imagination.

'Why not? You seem to think I'm capable of any depravity,' he declared mockingly.

'Not quite any . . .' she vouched with a smile, and burst out laughing as Nick dramatically flung the back of his hand across his brow.

'My God! A compliment. I can't believe it!'

'Cut out the play-acting, and stop trying to change the subject.'

'As if I would,' he leered and, wrapping his arms around her once more, he hugged her to his hard body, one hand gently stroking her hair as she lay with her head on his chest. For the first time since their remarriage they were totally at peace with each other.

'I did spend the night in my father's study. I sat at his desk, just thinking about him. All his life he hated his mother, and yet to anyone who knew them both it was glaringly obvious that they were exactly alike in nature and temperament. But he never saw it himself. It's funny how we never see ourselves as others do.'

'Quite the philosopher tonight,' Abby teased and, turning her head slightly, she bit lightly on a small, very masculine nipple. She felt the shudder that surged through him, and she laughed softly, delighting in his body's instant response.

'All right, woman, I can take a hint—enough of philosophy and down to some physiology,' he growled throatily. A second later she was flat on her back with Nick leaning over her, his grey eyes darkening with desire.

'I don't know what you mea-a-a-an,' she tried to tease, but it came out as a moan as his mouth closed over her breast.

He lifted his head, a devilish grin curving his sensuous mouth. 'It is that part of biology that deals with the functions of the human body, and I have to examine yours in minute detail,' he declared huskily, and proceeded to do just that. For the rest of the night the only sounds from the large bed were soft moans and muffled cries of pleasure.

Abby awoke to find Nick leaning over her, his face inches from hers. His lips sought hers in a kiss as soft as thistledown, and, still lingering in the afterglow of the wonderful night they had spent together, she parted her lips in a warm, dazzling smile. Nick groaned and straightened up, and it was then that she realised he was dressed in a severely cut black formal suit, and reality intruded.

'Sorry, Abby darling, but we haven't time.' The knowing gleam in his eyes brought a blush to her cheeks. 'It's going to be a hell of a day; the children will be here any minute. Marta has been taking care of them, but she wants to get ready. So . . .'

In a panic Abby shot out of bed, completely unconscious of her nudity until Nick caught her in his arms and crushed her mouth with his. His strong hands caressed her naked flesh from shoulder to thigh; every nerve-end in her body tingled at his touch, and she melted in his arms.

He lifted his head and smiled, a slow, triumphant, provoking smile that brought more colour to her cheeks. Then he groaned. 'What are you trying to do to me?'

She looked up into his face, but there was none of the mocking anger she had grown accustomed to. Nick was looking at her as though she was all the woman he had ever wanted. His silver-grey eyes were dark with desire and some other emotion she dared not put a name to. 'Last night was the most Elysian experience I have known in years, and at last I feel some confidence in our future together,' he opined hardily.

Her heart leapt with joy, 'Together?' she parroted. Was it possible? Dared she even contemplate a life with Nick?

'Oh, yes, my love. Definitely together.'

Their eyes locked and for a split second they laid bare their souls, each to the other. The doubt, the fear, the overwhelming desire.

'We need to talk, but not now. Tonight,' Nick husked, the word a promise.

CHAPTER NINE

FOR the next few hours Abby devoted all of her attention to the children. They had shared a hasty lunch in the kitchen at noon, by which time the place was full of the caterers hired to provide the meal for the funeral party. Afterwards she had shepherded them all into the big playroom at the rear of the house, out of everyone's way, and she couldn't help sighing with relief when a red-eyed but composed Catherine joined them at about four o'clock, telling Abby to go and make an appearance among the crowd of friends and business acquaintances who had returned with the family from the church.

In her own bedroom she quickly showered and changed into a slim-fitting black skirt and matching lambswool sweater, the only spot of colour a small gold embroidered butterfly on one shoulder. She brushed her long hair up into a neat chignon and, applying only a minimum of make up, she slipped her feet into black high-heeled court shoes, added a brief spray of her favourite perfume and she was ready.

She took one last look in the mirror and smiled rather guiltily. It was a sad, sombre occasion, and her reflected image was anything but. With her rich red hair, glowing skin and sparkling green eyes, she had never looked more vibrantly alive, and it was all Nick's doing. The chemical reaction between them had always been explosive from the very first day they had met in London, but last night had been a revelation; they had been closer in body and spirit than at any other time in their relationship. She loved Nick. To see him was to want him, the sound of his voice, his touch, made her heart tremble. There could never be any other man for her, and she had finally accepted the fact.

Abby left the bedroom, a secret smile playing around her lovely lips. She recalled Nick's words as they had parted this morning—'our future together'—and oh, how sweet they sounded!

She told herself to be realistic; one perfect night could not wipe away years of hurt and distrust. She had two choices. She could return to Cornwall with her son and forget the last few weeks—or she could stay in Greece. Nick desired her, that much she was sure of. His love for Jonathan was genuine, it was in his eyes every time he looked at the boy. She had changed over the past few years, so maybe so had he.

In the civilised world monogamy was growing in favour, the penalties for promiscuity too deadly to contemplate. Nick was an astute, intelligent man, so perhaps there was some hope for their marriage. As a young girl she had worshipped him, but now, older and more mature, her love for Nick was as deep and wide as the ocean he so feared. He was the father of her son, the keeper of her heart. The real question was, did she have the courage to face the future as his wife, while well aware of his propensity for straying? She didn't know. But hope soared as she made her decision—she was certainly going to try.

Abby reached the foot of the stairs and scanned the crowd of sombrely dressed visitors looking for her husband. She accepted the murmured condolences of a host of people, but the only one she actually knew was Dr Popodopoulos, a very talkative old man, and, as her last meeting with him in Athens had been on a rather sensitive subject, she excused herself politely before he could get into his stride. She wandered around the various rooms, but there was no sign of Nick. Finally she tried the study. The door swung open at her touch, and she stopped. Her fingers clenched around the door-knob, her knuckles gleaming white with the strain.

Nick was standing, his back towards her, his whole concentration centred on the small dark woman whose red-topped fingers were laced around his waist. 'I can't wait till next week, Nick. I am so happy. We have both finally got what we want.'

It was Melanie . . . Abby felt as though someone had

stuck a knife in her heart and sliced it into tiny pieces. All
the strength left her legs and for a horrible moment she
thought she was going to faint. Then she heard Nick speak.
'I probably shouldn't say it today of all days, but you're
right, Melanie, everything has turned out better than I dared
hope.'

Abby did not wait to hear any more; quietly she pulled
the door closed and walked away. Thank God they had not
seen her—at least she had been spared that humiliation. The
tearing pain subsided. It had to. No one could stand such
agony and live. Her heart once again encased in ice, she
drew on four years of practice and, tilting her chin, she fixed
a grim smile on her face and mingled with the guests. If
anyone noticed the bitter twist to her lips, or the blank,
expressionless look in her large eyes, they put it down to
grief at the death of her father-in-law and were suitably
sympathetic.

Abby almost laughed at the idiotic girl of half an hour
ago. Two choices—what a joke! There had never been a
choice to make. She had made the right decision four years
ago. She had too much pride to play the part of the
long-suffering wife. With luck she would be back in St Ives
in a few days, and hopefully all this would be just a bad
dream . . .

Abby's body tensed when she heard the bedroom door
open. She stayed seated at the dressing-table and
methodically carried on brushing her hair. She did not want
to look at Nick, she wasn't sure she could without
screaming abuse at him.

'Ready for bed, Abby, my love?' he asked.

With careful deliberation she placed the hairbrush on the
table and slowly raised her head to face his image in the
dressing-table mirror. Her breath locked in her throat as she
saw the flames of desire burning in his eyes. He was
stripped to the waist and his dark hair lay in tumbled locks
across his brow. He exuded a raw maleness, a powerful
masculinity that had an instant effect on her senses, but she
was determined to be the one in control, and, sliding off the
stool, she stood up. He reached for her arm, his intention

obvious. She took a step back, evading his hand.

'I believe you wanted to talk,' she prompted tonelessly, her pale face devoid of all expression. 'Personally I don't see that we have much to discuss. Catherine told me earlier that you are now the major shareholder in the company. So you have got what you want and I have fulfilled my part of our agreement. Jonathan and I will return to England on Monday,' she informed him through stiff lips.

'What the hell is the matter with you, Abby? Are you out of your mind?' Nick demanded, his mouth drawn in a tight angry line, as in one stride he closed the gap between them to tower menacingly over her.

Later she was to wonder if perhaps she had inherited some of her parents' acting ability, as she faced him coldly.

'Really, Nick, why the histrionics?' she drawled. 'Our agreement was quite clear, though I suppose for the sake of appearances we could wait till Tuesday,' she offered facetiously.

He went white about the mouth, and raised his hand; for a moment she thought he was going to strike her, but instead he ran his hand through his dark hair in an odd, almost defeated gesture. 'So we are back to square one, hmm?'

'I don't know what you mean,' she said, and wished he would just go. He was staring at her in the strangest manner and the atmosphere was incredibly tense. With a nervous gesture she fiddled with the belt of her towelling robe, her only garment.

'Nervous, Abby?' His glittering gaze dropped to her waist and then back to her face, his lips twisting derisively. She opened her mouth to deny it, but the words stuck in her throat. There was something in his expression that sent fear racing to every nerve-end in her body. 'Well, you bloody well should be!' He swore violently, and, dragging her into his arms, he brought his mouth down savagely, parting her quivering lips in angry possession. She could feel his fury in the pressure of his arms, they thudding beat of his heart, but for once her body remained numb.

'I could make you respond,' he gritted through clenched teeth, 'but I am getting heartily sick of your games, and am fast losing the desire to.' And, thrusting her from him, he stalked across the room.

'Good!' she snapped furiously at his broad back. He could not be half as sick as she was, she thought resentfully as the silence lengthened, gnawing away at Abby's nerves.

Nick turned slowly, and stood, his shoulders hunched, his hands thrust into his pockets, and regarded her in total silence, his features an inscrutable mask. Then he spoke in a voice devoid of any emotion. 'I left a warm, loving wife in this room this morning, and tonight I am greeted by a hard-faced stranger. Tell me, Abby, did last night mean anything at all to you?' he enquired sardonically.

'Good sex,' she managed to jeer. How dared he remind her of the wanton woman she had been the night before? It certainly hadn't meant anything to him, if today's episode in the study was anything to go by.

'Sex. It was more than that and you know it, but for some reason you refuse to admit it.' He took a step towards her, his grey eyes darkening with some emotion she could not define. 'I laid my soul bare to you last night, and you responded with everything that is in you. So why, Abby? Tell me why? I want to understand. You're my wife, for God's sake!'

For a second she almost believed he was sincere, and she was tempted to tell him the truth—that she had seen him with Melanie—and demand an explanation, but common sense prevailed. She knew he would mockingly dismiss her jealousy now, as he had done in the past, leaving her hurt and humiliated. So she bitterly attacked him in the one way guaranteed to hurt him. 'Why? That is simple enough to answer,' she said, not bothering to disguise her enmity. 'I felt sorry for you.'

For an instant she thought he was going to kill her, so great was his rage. She knew she had gone too far. To a man like Nick, pity was intolerable. Her green eyes wide with fear, she watched his struggle to retain control. The blood drained from his face leaving it white, almost skeletal. A nerve jumping spasmodically in her cheek betrayed the effort of will it took to thrust her away and say in a deadly quiet voice, 'You can leave when you like.'

She should have been exultant that she had at last smashed his massive ego, but instead she felt curiously deflated.

'Thank you. I'll ring the airline tomorrow,' she said softly.

'Just one ticket, Abby. You go alone.' He turned on his heel and walked towards the bathroom without a backward glance.

'No, you can't do that!' she cried as the import of his words sank in. Impulsively she followed him into the bathroom. 'Jonathan stays with me. He has to. We had an agreement, you promised. It was understood that when your father died Jonathan and I would be free.' She was babbling, but didn't seem able to stop. Nick could not be serious.

'You really should learn to be more specific, my dear. You did not say that at the time,' he informed her silkily. He was right, she had not mentioned his father, but he had known very well what she had meant. 'But I can't leave without Jonathan.' She searched his face for any sign of weakness. She was trembling with shock, her heart pumping ice through her veins. At the back of her mind she had always feared he had some ulterior motive. He wanted her son . . . Never! He could not do this to her. 'You can't keep me here,' she wailed her eyes skidding helplessly over his near naked body as he casually stepped out of his trousers.

'There are no chains or locks,' Nick drawled mockingly, and proceeded to remove his last garment, black briefs.

'I'll take him anyway,' she declared defiantly, but her senses reeled as he straightened up, his superb body stark naked, and her face went hot as the male scent of him tormented her.

'There is no way you can take him. The boy is registered on my passport, and as for you . . .' glacial eyes bored down into hers pitilessly '. . . the decision is entirely yours. I find I no longer care one way or the other.' And, opening the shower door, he added cynically, 'If my body disturbs you, don't worry. When we return to Athens you can sleep in the guest-room. I would prefer it that way.'

Abby stood rooted to the spot, staring vacantly at the closed door. How had it all gone so wrong?

'I know it's none of my business, but I am going to have my say. It isn't right, not right at all, you sleeping in the guest-room. Nr Nick is all man, he needs his wife in his bed. You're just making trouble for yourself, mark my words,' Mary informed Abby bluntly.

They had returned to this 'dream house' ten days ago, and they had been the worst ten days of Abby's life. She sighed, and, draining her coffee-cup, put it down on the table. Jonathan was becoming a real problem—for the past week he had been irritable and very naughty. This morning he had refused to go to school and it had taken the persuasive powers of Mary, Henry and herself to get him in the car. She could not find it in her heart to blame him. He adored his father and in the last ten days Nick had barely spent half an hour with the boy.

It was like a re-run of a bad movie, Abby thought hopelessly. Her husband returned late at night, or, as last night, not at all. No wonder Jonathan was upset.

Mary's voice rang with a sternness that would have done a sergeant major credit. 'You love the man, so why carry on this stupid argument or whatever it is? You need your head read, my girl.'

Abby cringed; were her feelings really so obvious? And, jumping to her feet, she said cuttingly, 'You're right, Mary, it is none of your business,' and walked out of the kitchen. She knew she had upset the older woman, but she couldn't help it. The trouble was it hurt too much. She loved Nick and it was killing her by inches to live in the same house with him, knowing he didn't give a damn about her. At night she lay in her lonely bed, aching for his touch . . .

The chiming of the doorbell interrupted her tortuous thoughts, and, crossing the hall, she opened the door to a flushed and tearful Jonathan in the arms of one of the teachers from the nursery school. She whisked him upstairs and in a matter of minutes he was bathed and safely tucked in bed. Seemingly he had been violently sick at school and spots were noticed on his little legs, so the principal had thought it advisable to send him straight home.

'Chicken-pox,' Mary declared confidently, and to Abby, sitting on the bed gently bathing her son's flushed face with a damp cloth, it sounded like the black plague. Jonathan had never been ill in his short life, and it tore at her heart to see his usually sparkling eyes so dull and listless.

Abby looked up at Mary. 'Are you sure?' she asked, badly needing reassurance. The doctor had been called immediately but as yet had not arrived.

''Course I am. Calamine lotion and cotton gloves to stop him scratching, that's what he needs, 'Mary said succinctly, then added artfully, 'There's nothing like that in the first-aid box. You will have to ring Mr Kardis and tell him to bring the lotion back with him, and don't forget the gloves.'

Reluctantly Abby went next door to her own room and picked up the telephone—she had not rung Nick at his office in years, mainly because she had no desire to speak to Melanie. But it was an emergency and she had no excuse.

At first she thought Nick must have changed his number as a young man's voice answered, 'Stavros speaking,' but he quickly enlightened her—he was Mr Kardis's new secretary of some two months' standing. She had no time to study the implications of the information as Nick's voice came cold and distant over the wire. 'Yes, what do you want, Abby?' Hurriedly she explained the situation, while unable to quell the sharp stab of pleasure the sound of his voice evoked.

'Right, I'll get everything that is needed and be straight there, and don't worry, Abby,' he commanded toughly. She was still holding the telephone receiver long after Nick had cut the connection, her mind a mass of confusing thoughts. Nick had a new secretary—but why? Where was Melanie? Had Nick fired her? No . . . That was impossible. They were still close, she had seen it with her own eyes at the funeral. Jonathan's pitiful cry of 'Mummy' intruded and quickly she replaced the telephone and went back to her son's bedside. The doctor arrived a few minutes later and there was no time to wonder about Melanie or anything else.

It was a young assistant of Dr Popodopoulos, the older man being away for a few days, she was informed. The doctor confirmed Mary's diagnosis, wrote a prescription for a mild analgesic for the fever and irritability, and had just left when Nick came bounding up the stairs and into the room.

'Have you had chicken-pox?' he curtly demanded of Abby, and when she answered in the affirmative he nodded and proceeded to ignore her completely, his whole attention focused on Jonathan. Within minutes he had the little boy smiling, albeit weakly.

Standing looking down at the two males so close together, and so obviously in tune with each other, Abby was filled with regret for what might have been. She felt like a spare wheel, excluded, and suddenly she could take no more.

'I'll go and make coffee,' she mumbled and, with a watery smile for Jonathan, she hastened out of the room.

'What the hell were you thinking of, sending the boy to school in that state?'

The words flicked Abby like a whip across her shoulders; she had not heard Nick walk into the kitchen. She sat up straighter in the hard-backed chair, tension in every line of her body as she lifted her head to meet his angry gaze.

'Perhaps if you had been home in the last thirty-six hours you could have done better,' she responded sarcastically, loath to admit he had some justification for his question.

'Forget I said that. It's not your fault.' And, walking across the room, he pulled out a chair and sat down at the table. 'Is there any coffee in the pot?'

Nick's apology stunned Abby into silence.

'God! I'm tired. I fell asleep at the office last night, and not with some dolly-bird, as no doubt your fertile imagination concluded,' he drawled mockingly. Then, raising one hand, he yawned widely.

Abby busied herself pouring out his coffee, but she chanced a quick glance at his face. He did look tired, she thought. His hard-boned face was thinner, lines of strain fanned out from his shadowed eyes, and for the first time she realised the past few weeks could not have been easy for Nick. She had always thought of him as a rock, indomitable, a man nothing could hurt, but she knew that wasn't true. He had proved his vulnerability that memorable night on the eve of his father's funeral, and, because of Melanie, Abby had deliberately squashed the knowledge, but now she was tormented by doubts. She handed him the coffee-cup and flinched as their fingers touched. It had been so long since she had felt the touch of his hand, the warmth of his hold, and loving him as she did she was terrified of betraying her need. 'How is Jonathan?' she blurted.

'He is all right. Mary is with him.' Nick's grey eyes gleamed knowingly into hers, fully aware of her reaction.

'Celibacy becoming a strain, Abby?' he asked silkily. 'Well, you know where my room is, and the door is never locked. Who knows, you might get lucky, but not tonight—I'm shattered.' Abby went from red to white to red again, and Nick laughed.

She felt like throwing her coffee all over his laughing face, but she forced herself to ignore his deliberate taunt. 'I won't grace that comment with an answer,' she told him with some dignity. 'Our son is ill, and the last thing he needs in his parents arguing.'

'You're right,' Nick sighed, his harsh features relaxing in a glimmer of smile—the first Abby had seen in weeks, and her lips quirked in a tentative response.

The episode in the kitchen seemed to herald a change in Nick's attitude. His former indifference gave way to a cautious concern, and to Abby's bruised heart it was a small but hopeful sign. He spent a lot of time on the phone, but never went to the office; instead he paid a lot of attention to Jonathan, sitting with him for hours at a time.

Abby found herself studying Nick secretly at every opportunity. She was dying to ask him about Melanie, but was too afraid to do so. She was terrified of revealing the true state of her feelings. Her furious anger at what she had thought was yet another betrayal had dissipated, and she was left with the gnawing doubt that maybe . . . just maybe she had acted too hastily because of one overheard conversation. Her fierce jealousy, a destructive emotion she had not realised she was capable of, might have cost her her one chance at a happy marriage. The insidious thought would not go away. What if Nick had been referring to his new relationship with her, and she had deliberately destroyed it by telling him she pitied him? Abby had to know, but ruefully she admitted she had not the courage to ask.

Jonathan's illness had eased the tension between them. It was amazing that a sick child could achieve in minutes what had been impossible before—a softening in Nick's behaviour—and she didn't want to upset the unspoken but real truce between Nick and herself.

After dinner the next night, Abby was lounging in the sitting-room, a glass of much-needed wine in her hand. Thankfully Jonathan was much better, the only sign of his illness the sixty-four spots—he kept counting, or demanding someone else did—and it was taking all Abby's powers of inventiveness, along with those of every other adult in the house, to keep the boy amused.

The door opened, interrupting her thoughts, and Nick walked in. She noticed he had removed his jacket and tie since dinner, and only one button remained fastened on his shirt. Her eyes wandered over the magnificent male length of him as he lowered himself casually into the chair opposite, his long legs stretched out in front of him, his dark head tipped back against the plump cushions in an attitude of complete relaxation. She wasn't aware she was staring until a mocking voice asked softly, 'Have I got two heads or something?'

The words pierced her heart, a vivid reminder of their first meeting at the Ritz. Only now she did not have the courage to tease back. A flush spread up her throat, and she could not look at him. 'No,' she mumbled into her glass, and drained the liquid.

'No. So why the scrutiny?' he demanded hardly.

She raised her head and was caught and held by the

intensity of his silvery gaze. 'Why is Melanie no longer your secretary?' She said the first thing that came into her head, and immediately wished she could take the words back as his lips quirked in a cynical smile. But to her surprise he answered her quite gravely.

'Melanie was a very efficient secretary, but unfortunately she rather carelessly betrayed my trust, so I promoted her to a position more suitable to her attributes and where she can do no harm.'

Oh!' Abby said, totally ineptly. Looking at her very masculine husband, who, even tired and only partly dressed, exuded an aura of ruthless arrogance that would make a hardened businessman tremble, she could almost feel sorry for the poor woman. Until she realised perhaps he thought the position of mistress more in keeping with her attributes, and her heart sank.

'Oh!' he parroted, his lips twisting in a derisive smile. 'What's that puritanical little mind of yours imagining now? That I've set Melanie up in a love nest, hmm?' The bright colour in her cheeks told him more plainly than words that he had guessed right.

'No, no, of course not,' Abby denied, while cursing his ability to read her mind so easily. She shrank back in her seat as he stood up and in one lithe stride towered over her. He clasped her chin between his finger and thumb, tilting her face up to his, so she could not evade the compelling intensity of his gaze. She shivered involuntarily at his touch, but with a great effort of will she clamped down on her body's wayward response to his nearness and bravely held his gaze.

'In any relationship, business or private, trust is the most essential ingredient,' he said hardly, then, letting go of her chin, he straightened and added enigmatically, 'You should try it some time, Abby. You might be pleasantly surprised at the results.' And, turning on his heel, he left.

'Trust.' Abby could not believe the hypocrisy of the man. Was he actually suggesting she trust him? After all that had gone before? No. It wasn't possible, he was just being his usual sarcastic self, but honesty forced her to admit he had sounded not sarcastic but deadly serious.

Hours later, lying in her lonely bed, she was still going over the conversation in her mind, unable to sleep. Did Nick want her to trust him? Could she? Dared she even try? They were questions she found hard to answer, but one thing was certain—she could not spend the next fifteen years or so living with Nick in a state of armed truce. She would be a nervous wreck or worse. She loved Nick, and God, how she wanted him! she thought, tossing restlessly in the bed. Surely they could reach a compromise for living together that would satisfy them both? Finally she came to a decision, just before sleep claimed her. If what she suspected was true, she had no choice: she had to swallow her pride and try to make their marriage work.

The next morning Abby dressed with more care than usual in a soft jade lambswool sweater and a matching, hip-hugging skirt that flared gently round her calves. She had no plan in mind, but was trusting instinct to guide her. She hurried into Jonathan's bedroom, and her heart slammed against her ribs as she collided with Nick coming out. He automatically reached out to steady her, and for a moment she wallowed in the luxury of being in his arms once more; the clean male scent of him, the feel of his muscular chest beneath her palms, made her blood surge in an instant response. But it was short-lived . . .

'Excuse me,' Nick said, and lifted her to one side.

'You're going out?'

He was dressed in an immaculate pearl-grey business suit and a snowy white shirt with a co-ordinating simple striped silk tie, and to Abby he looked devastating. He arched one dark brow enquiringly. 'Why does it matter to you?' he drawled cynically.

'Jonathan,' she said, then mindful of her decision of the previous night, she added bravely, 'Yes. Will you be back for dinner?' It was a stupid, stupid question, she knew. But her nerve had failed her at the last minute.

'So mundane a question. You sound like a wife, Abby.' And, raising one hand, he lightly tapped her cheek. 'One day you will say what you mean, but in the meantime, yes,

I will be back for dinner.' And, brushing a few stray curls from her brow, he pressed his lips to her forehead and walked away.

Abby was stunned for all of two minutes, and it was only when Jonathan called, 'Mummy!' that she turned to look at his little body curled up on the bed, and she realised sadly that Nick had probably kissed her for his son's benefit and nothing else. Still, she told herself, it was the first hint she had had in two weeks that Nick might care a little for her, and, settling down on the bed, she prepared to amuse her son.

The arrival of Dr Popodopoulos in the afternoon was a welcome break from trying to amuse a very active Jonathan, and Abby was delighted to listen to the old man's chatter for a change. He examined Jonathan and declared him as fit as could be expected, considering the boy looked like a spotted Dick. Which led to a long story about the old man's days at Oxford in the distant past, where he had acquired a taste for the currant puddings. It was as Abby was seeing him out that the doctor dropped his bombshell.

Standing on the doorstep, he reassured her once again that Jonathan would be fine and added, 'Of course, he almost certainly caught it from Catherine's youngest. I saw the child last week, and the spots were just beginning to fade. Mind you, that horde of Catherine's is pretty lethal. They have had every childhood illness known to man, and some twice over.' He chuckled reminiscently. 'I remember when the two eldest had mumps, years ago. They very nearly unmanned their poor Uncle Nick.'

Abby's eyes widened in surprise. 'Nick?' she said curiously.

'Yes. He got the mumps. It wasn't funny—not for a man his age. Oh, it must have been what? Over a year later I did some tests, and I was sure he was sterile. But we all make mistakes, and thank God that little chap upstairs proved me wrong, hmm?' And with that he left.

Numb, her mind reeling with shock, Abby staggered across the entrance hall to the foot of the stairs. 'Mary,' she called, 'I'm going to my studio. Look after Jonathan,

please.' She needed to be alone. She could not believe what
she had heard; the implications were too horrific.

'Are you all right, girl?'

'Yes, yes, I'm fine,' she flung over her shoulder as she
ascended the stairs. There was no way she could face
anyone. If it was true, God, the wasted years, the
unnecessary pain—it couldn't be true... Could it...?

CHAPTER TEN

ABBY walked into the studio and collapsed on the black hide sofa, her head falling back, her eyes closed. The enormity of the doctor's revelation was too much for her seething brain to assimilate, and yet she knew deep down that the old man had told the truth. He had no reason to lie . . .

How long she simply lay there she never knew, but gradually the ordinary sounds of the house—a door closing, voices raised in laughter—brought her mind back to reality. She groaned and slowly opened her eyes, dazedly looking around the room. Her studio. A present from her husband. Oh, lord! What had she done? a voice screamed in her head. A hundred little instances suddenly made appalling sense, like the pieces of a giant jigsaw fitting together, and she cringed with shame at her own horrifying blind, selfish stupidity.

Painfully she acknowledged that all the information had been there from the very start of their relationship, and she had been too insensitive to see it. The day at the zoo, Nick had told her he had been ill after visiting his sister. That must have been the time the doctor meant. She remembered the first twelve happy months of marriage, when she had never doubted Nick's love. He had treated her like a queen, spoiled and indulged her. Anything she'd wanted, he'd given her. It was only after that fateful Christmas, when she had happily told him there was no reason why she shouldn't have a child, that their relationship had collapsed, and now she knew why. Nick had discovered the one thing she wanted above all else, a child, and he had thought he was incapable of giving her one. He had admitted as much when he'd asked her to marry him again, and she had dismissed his story as just a convenient lie . . .

Her heart ached for him. He was such a proud man. What

167

it must have cost him to know, or even think, he was sterile.
Looking back to the last months before they parted,
suddenly she saw that his actions made a macabre kind of
sense. She had sat there with her temperature charts,
waffling on about the optimim time to conceive, while he
must have been dying inside. His father's constant carping
about pregnancy had irritated the younger Abby, but it must
have been a thousand times worse for Nick. No wonder he
had reacted so violently the one time she had cast a slur on
his virility. How could she have been so dense? All those
months when he'd been moody, irritable, totally unlike his
usual self, not once had it occurred to her to ask him if there
was anything medically wrong. Instead she had
immediately assumed he had another woman. True, he had
encouraged her in that belief but as his wife she should have
looked deeper, understood him better. Looking back at the
girl she had been, Abby ruefully admitted she was more her
parents' daughter than she had ever realised. She had
play-acted her way from art student to model to perfect
wife, and, when harsh reality had intruded on her ideal, she
had not known how to handle it.

With hindsight she could recognise that her intuition had
been right. She had hung on to her marriage for so long
because she had not been able to believe Nick did not love
her. Was it possible he had loved her too much?

She had accused him of being unfaithful, of lying to her,
but in retrospect she realised he had never admitted to being
unfaithful in so many words. It had all been suggestion—a
photo in the papers, gossip—and the ending of the intimate
side of their relationship had convinced her. True, he had
paraded the actress friend before her at that fatal party. But
surely only an incredibly stupid man would allow his
mistress to gatecrash such an important social event, and
Nick was anything but a fool . . .

Abby slowly got to her feet and walked across to the
easel in the centre of the room. The canvas upon it was a
partly finished portrait of Jonathan, the third she had
attempted. Her lips twisted in a wry smile. She had made
the same mistake again: the child's features had become

those of a much older man. Nick . . .

As Abby gazed at the portrait she felt hope blossom and unfurl in her heart like the first flower of spring. Before, the possibility of Nick's loving her had been so remote that she had considered his ruthless attitude towards her to be purely for selfish gain, to be despicable, and God knew she had argued with him enough about it. But now she realised he had some excuse for his deep-rooted anger. Starkly it hit her. Nick must have thought the child she had borne was not his . . .

In a fever of anticipation she waited for Nick to come home. They had a lot of explaining to do, but this time Abby vowed she would listen and trust him—something she should have done weeks ago. It wouldn't be easy, but the way she felt now she would get down on her knees and beg if she had to. She loved him so much, and a lifetime of happiness was at stake.

The trouble was, she thought bitterly a few hours later, Nick had not given her the chance. He had returned from the office and with a curt greeting to Abby had gone straight to Jonathan, making it obvious that her presence was not required. Now, sitting twiddling her thumbs at the dinner table, she wished he would hurry up and join her. In an attempt to bolster her confidence she had spent ages bathing and dressing with care. She knew she looked good—the gown she was wearing was a John Galliano creation in green chiffon, with an intricately tucked bodice that fitted snugly to a broad-belted waist, the skirt a figure-hugging deeper green that flared out in a stepped hem ending at her knees. It had been her one wild extravagance last year, bought to attend a special dinner for the Lord Lieutenant of the county, and she had never worn it since.

'Waiting for me? There was no need,' Nick said tersely, not sparing her a glance as he strolled across the room and, pulling out a chair, sat down at the table. Immediately he helped himself to a plate full of steak and vegetables and proceeded to eat.

Abby watched him with mounting anger. She knew it was unreasonable, but she couldn't help it. He looked so self-contained and devastatingly attractive in a plain navy roll-necked sweater and cream trousers. Usually dinner was a formal meal. Why, tonight, did he have to choose to dress casually? Briefly she wondered if he had done it deliberately, then dismissed the thought as unworthy. He could not have known she would go to the other extreme. She felt stupidly over-dressed.

'Not hungry?' he asked and, looking across at her, lifted his dark brows sardonically. 'You're looking very glamorous. Are you going somewhere?'

'No,' she muttered, feeling the colour flood her face, and hastily she served herself with a small portion of food, with a hand that wasn't quite steady. This wasn't going at all as she had envisaged.

'Rather overdoing it, aren't you?' he mocked, eyeing the emerald necklace she had rashly worn in the hope it would remind him of happier times. 'Christmas isn't for another couple of weeks,' he added with a chuckle.

'Thank you,' she snapped. So he thought she looked like a Christmas tree. She breathed deeply and counted to ten. Losing her temper with him was not what she had intended. Ruefully she admitted she had used anger to mask her true feelings for far too long; it was becoming a habit, and anyway he was probably right. 'Nick,' she said hesitantly 'I saw Dr——Popodopoulos today, and he told me. Well . . . he said that——'

'Nothing wrong with Jonathan, is there?' he swiftly interrupted, concern evident in his tone.

'No. No, he's fine.' And, nervously meeting his eyes, she simply blurted out, 'He told me you had mumps, and the tests you took, and everything . . .'She ground to a halt as his features became an expressionless mask.

'So what's new?' he drawled.

'Why didn't you tell me?' she demanded, her voice rising in agitation.

'As I recall, I did. Months ago.' He rose abruptly, and his derisive glance held hers as he methodically folded his napkin and placed it on the table. 'It's all water under the bridge, Abby. Forget it. I have.'

He was gone before she could protest, leaving Abby unhappily wondering how the future that had looked so promising a few hours ago could once again look so black. No. She would not give up so easily, and, jumping up, she chased after him. 'No, you don't understand,' she cried, and he paused at the foot of the stairs to glance back at her with cool indifference. 'I meant . . .' Her heart beat rapidly as she struggled to find the words, her eyes feasting on his tall, dominant figure draped casually against the newel post.

'You meant?' he prompted silkily.

What did she mean? She did not know. How could she say to him, I love you, and I think you might love me, when he was looking at her as if she were something unpleasant that had crawled out from under a rock. 'You don't understand,' she repeated, while her mind searched frantically for a way to explain.

'I understand perfectly,' he sneered. 'You believe the good doctor, Melanie—almost anyone other than me, your husband. Well, don't let it worry you. I've got used to it. Now, if you will excuse me, I'm going to have an early night.'

'No, please wait,' she said, and, reaching out, she grabbed his arm. Nick looked insolently down at her slender fingers curved around his forearm, and she trembled as the warmth of his flesh through the fine wool of his sweater sent shock-waves of electricity darting up her arm. Aware of her reaction, he raised mocking eyes to hers.

'Wait? What for?' he asked cynically, a semblance of a smile twisting his mouth as he glanced down at her full breasts straining against the soft chiffon of her dress. Her body responded with lightning rapidity, her breasts growing taut against the soft fabric. Her face and her body burnt with colour, but this time she made no effort to hide her reaction. She told herself she had to take a chance. She had been a coward far too long.

'Nick, I want to try and make our marriage work. If you will help me?' she asked in a rush. Then she held her breath, mentally willing him to say yes, to accept the olive branch she offered. She caught a flash of—was it caution?—in his hard, narrowed eyes, and then to her amazement he swung her up into his arms. Frantically she wrapped her own slender arms around his bronzed neck to prevent herself from falling as he ascended the stairs two at a time.

Her lips were only inches from his smoothly shaven cheek. The musky male scent of him, the heat of his muscular body hard against her own aroused a traitorous warmth, an aching longing inside her, a fierce need to feel once more the full passionate force of his possession. It had been so long. Too long, she thought fervently, and as she felt his mouth nuzzle lightly against her throat she flung back her head, exposing the elegant line of her neck to his sweetly tormenting lips. She reeled under the impact of the sensations his gentle caresses aroused in her, and barely registered his belated reply.

'Yes, why not? Sexual frustration is hell, isn't it, my darling wife?'

There was something not quite right about his words, but Abby was too bemused to think. She clung to him as he slowly lowered her down the hard length of his body. There was no mistaking the hardness of his arousal against her and she shivered with delight that she could still affect him so instantly. Her feet barely touched the ground when he threaded his long fingers through her shining golden hair and brought his mouth down on her softly parted lips in a kiss of hard, bruising passion. Her body arched into his and willingly she gave in to his long, drugging kisses. Dropping his large hands to her shoulders, he broke the kiss and gently eased her away from him. She took great dragging breaths, trying to get some air back in her lungs, and made no demur when Nick rasped, 'Take off your clothes, Abby,' and led the way by stripping his sweater over his head.

First she removed the emeralds and dropped them on the dressing-table, then, more slowly, she unbuckled her belt and allowed the soft chiffon to float to the floor. Without Nick's arms around her, she suddenly felt unsure, and she hesitated, her fingers on the front clasp of her bra. Her eyes focused on Nick, her gaze moving over his near naked torso. This was what she wanted, wasn't it?

There was no more time for doubt. He removed his pants and when he straightened up she met the smouldering darkness of his gaze and her bones melted. The slight disquiet she had felt vanished like smoke in the wind.

'Let me help you,' he drawled huskily, reaching out to her.

She felt his body close to hers, and she ached to be closer to him. She trembled as he deftly removed her bra, and when his long fingers sought the top of her lacy briefs she helped him remove them with an unconscious erotic wriggle of her hips. They melded together, satin skin to silk, mouth to mouth, fusing together as though they were made for one another, two halves of a whole.

'Nick,' she breathed, hungrily, as he lifted her in his arms and laid her on the wide bed. To touch, to taste, to love him was her one desire. He filled up her senses, until she was drunk on the wonder of him. His huge body arched over her, his eyes glittered down into hers, and then his head swooped down, taking her mouth once more.

His hands slid sensuously over her body, while his mouth burnt a white-hot trail of fire to her swollen breasts. She groaned as he found the rigid peaks, and traced the darker aureoles with his tongue before devouring them with his mouth. She cried out, and her back arched involuntarily, seeking more, while her fingers dug into his wide shoulders.

'God, but I want this. I can't wait,' Nick groaned, his voice thick with a hunger that Abby felt herself.

There was a new violence, a driven urgency about Nick that awakened the same response in her, and when his strong hand caressed the curve of her hips and lifted her she was more than ready for him. Twining her legs around his waist, she whimpered as he thrust into her. Their bodies joined in a wild, primeval rhythm neither could control. Her nails raked his back as the tension inside her was stretched almost to torture-point, to explode in surge after surge of ecstasy, more devastating than anything she had ever experienced before. Nick's savage cry of triumph as his

great body shuddered in release together with her own
echoed Abby's breathless, broken scream.

Eyes closed, Abby felt totally satiated and complete for
the first time in years. She opened her eyes, and cradled
Nick's head in her arms. He was slumped over her, his face
buried in the hollow of her throat, and a rush of love and
compassion swept over her, so powerful that it brought a
lump to her throat. A long-drawn-out sigh of blessed relief
escaped her. The tension, the wall of anger and bitterness
she had built to protect her own vulnerability had crumbled
to dust. She felt oddly light-headed, rejoicing in the weight
of Nick's sweat-slicked body pinning her to the bed. This
magnificent male animal was her husband, and by his
passion verging on madness he had shown her more clearly
than words that he had accepted her tentative offer of a
normal marriage.

She listened to the shuddering rasp of his breathing, her
fingers sliding lovingly into the damp curl of his hair,
brushing it back from his proud forehead. Surely he must
love her? Thank God, she thought, and, 'Thank you, my
darling,' she murmured softly. She couldn't be mistaken
again. But she was . . .

Nick lifted his head and stared down at her with
curiously blank eyes. 'No need to thank me,' he drawled
and, rolling off her, he added, 'I told you before, my door
is always open and I am happy to oblige.'

Abby froze for a second at the flat, indifferent tone of his
voice, but her heart could not believe what she heard.
Frantically she made excuses for him; he must have
misunderstood something she had said. In a voice that
trembled on the edge of panic, she told him, 'Nick, we have
to talk. I meant what I told you earlier, I want to be your
wife in every way. I'm truly sorry about the past, but——'

'Shut up, Abby. I'm tired, I want to go to sleep, and the
last thing I need is your pity,' he said curtly, and turned his
back on her.

Pity. Was that what he thought? She reached out a hand
towards him. 'Please, Nick,' she whispered. She could not
leave it like this. She needed to tell him that she loved him,

and that pity had nothing to do with it. She had hurt him before. They had hurt each other. But surely the last hour had proved to him that she had changed, now she knew the truth? She tried again, her fingers trembling on his smoothly muscled back. 'Nick——' But he ignored her, and within minutes the deep, even tone of his breathing told her he was asleep.

The tears she had restrained for so long filled her eyes and spilled over to trickle slowly down her soft cheeks. She couldn't help it. The trauma of the last few hours had finally torn down all her defences, and Nick's callous comment had left her heart raw and bleeding. She made a feeble attempt to mask her sobs by burying her face in the pillow, but her whole body shook with the force of her desolation. Nick did not love her; he never had. Why? Why me, Lord? her mind screamed. What have I ever done so terrible to deserve such heartbreak? And, with no answer to the endless question, she gave in to a paroxysm of tears.

With a string of muttered curses Nick turned over and hauled her into his arms. 'Oh, hell! Abby, I can't bear to hear you cry,' he said thickly, but she didn't hear him. 'Hush, Abby, don't.' With one strong hand he stroked her naked back, while his other smoothed her tumbled mass of silky hair. 'I'm sorry if I hurt you, if I was too rough, but damn it! You make me that way,' he groaned.

But she was too far gone to respond. Long shudders racked her slender frame and, with her head buried on his broad chest, her tears ran free, to mingle with his softly curling body hair. 'Please, sweetheart, you'll make yourself ill.'

Didn't he know she *was* ill? her heart cried out to him. Ill with a fatal disease she could never recover from. She had tried so hard to pretend she didn't care, to hate him. but it was no good, she couldn't pretend any more. 'I love you and it hurts. It hurts so much,' she choked almost incoherently. Stripped of all pride, and violent in her grief, her small fists beat furiously against him, as she broke down completely.

For a long moment, as though stunned, Nick let her go

wild, then with a ruthless ease he captured her wrists in one large hand and held them pinned to his chest. Abby wriggled in a futile attempt at freedom, but his heavy thighs trapped her slender body between his long legs, and she was held immobile, sprawled on top of him.

'Stop it. Stop it,' he commanded harshly.

Her tears eased; they had to, for she had cried herself dry. With her forearms resting on his chest, she looked down into his darkly flushed face. The silvery moonlight, cutting a swathe across the wide bed, played tricks with her senses, as through tear-drenched lashes she imagined she saw for a second Nick's grey eyes glistened with moisture. But that could not be . . . 'I—I can't h-help it,' she hiccuped, her full lips swollen and trembling. 'I can't take any more,' she confessed. 'Your coldness, your polite indifference.' She stared at him, the love, the pain plain to see in the anguished expression on her beautiful face. 'I'm sorry,' she whispered sadly, gradually regaining her senses and ashamed of her hysterical outburst.

'Sorry?' Nick lifted a finger and gently traced the path of a last solitary tear down her soft cheek. 'You have nothing to apologise for,' he declared, his deep voice oddly unsteady.

Her long lashes fluttered over her cheeks. He was trying to be kind, she knew, and she could not bear his kindness. She wanted so much more . . . Then his hand tangled in her long hair, pulling her head back, the better to see her face, and his dark eyes locked on hers as if they would see into her very soul.

'You said you loved me. Did you mean it?' he demanded hardly. 'Or are you confusing love with pity?'

'Pity? If I pity anyone it's myself,' Abby acknowledged with brutal honesty. 'I love you, Nick, I always have, and always will.' What was the point of prevaricating? she thought forlornly. Her hysterical breakdown had already told him the truth.

'Are you sure?' he rasped, and she felt his muscular body lock with tension as he waited for her response.

'Very, very sure.'

'Oh, God, Abby, I love you too,' he groaned, his arms tightening convulsively around her yielding body. He buried his face in the fragrant glory of her hair. 'If only you knew how long I have wanted and waited to hear you say again that you love me. I had almost lost hope.' His lips sought hers and he kissed her with an aching, bitter-sweet tenderness that stole her breath away.

Incredulous hope grew and grew in her heart. 'You love me?' she whispered, hardly daring to believe it was true, and, pressing her small hands flat against his chest, she eased away from him and warily stared down at him. The expression in his eyes nearly stopped her heart, so full of love and tenderness that it was almost painful.

'Don't ever doubt it, Abby. I should never have let you go. I loved you too much, and I wanted to give you the world.' A faint grimace curved his lips. 'And in my conceit I thought I could.'

'Oh, Nick, all I ever wanted was you.' She gave him a wry smile. 'I know I was a bit neurotic about having a baby, but mostly because I thought it was what you wanted, and your father, he——'

'No, Abby.' He stopped her with a finger over her mouth 'It wasn't your fault. I was entirely to blame. You can't imagine what it did to me, thinking I could never be a father. I felt half a man, useless.' His dark eyes clouded with remembered pain, and consolingly Abby stroked his broad shoulders, feeling his anguish as if it were her own. 'God, I idolised you. I still do,' he said throatily, replacing the finger on her lips with a brief kiss. 'But in those days I was stupidly noble, and also slightly off my head. My male ego was so shattered I couldn't think straight. I deliberately chased you away. I hurt you, and you're the last person in the world I should have hurt! His grey eyes clouded with uncertainty, he asked, 'Can you ever forgive me, Abby?'

Heart to heart, wrapped in the comfort of his arms, she pressed her lips to the hollow in his throat and murmured softly, 'I'll forgive you anything just so long as you keep on loving me.' Her body tingled with renewed awareness and she writhed sensuously against him, feeling the stirring in his loins. A secret smile tilted her lovely mouth.

'I don't deserve you,' Nick groaned, and for a long time explanations were forgotten as their open mouths met and clung with blind, ravishing hunger and something more than passion: total commitment, an avowal of love.

Nick's large hands spanned her waist and lifted her, laying her on her back. She reached up to him, her slender fingers lacing around the back of his neck, the blood pounding violently through her body in exultant anticipation. Lifting heavy lashes, she met his eyes. His were black with passion but oddly strained, his jaw clenched as if he was in pain, and as she would have pulled him down to her he groaned and jerkily disentangled her hands from his nape. 'No, Abby,' he said hoarsely. 'First we must talk.' His massive chest heaved with the effort of will it took to put some space between them, and, lying on his side, he supported his weight on one elbow and looked down at her flushed face and misty green eyes glazed with desire.

'Later, Nick. We can talk later,' she tempted, all woman, sensuous and seductive, but he would not be deterred.

'No, sweetheart,' he grinned wryly. 'I dare not. That night in Corfu I thought we would talk later, and look what happened. I've suffered two weeks of sheer hell. This time I am not touching you until everything is perfectly clear. I want no more misunderstandings.'

Abby knew he was right, but still she edged closer to him, and slid one slender arm around his back. Her other hand gently fondled the curly black hair of his chest, and her gaze slid down the sexy male length of him, his flat belly and muscular thighs. She marvelled at his self-control as her eyes lingered on the rigid perfection of his masculinity. Nick chuckled and swiftly pulled the soft sheet halfway up their bodies. 'Stop looking at me like that, woman,' he growled. 'I'm trying to be serious.'

'Sorry.' She smiled, raising her eyes to his face, and snuggling closer still.

'Yes, well, where was I?' He cleared his throat. 'After you left I kept telling myself I had done the right thing, but it didn't make losing you any easier. Then, the day you told me on the phone you were pregnant, I went crazy with anger. All I could think of was, it hadn't taken you five minutes to find someone else, while I couldn't look at another woman. God, what a prize idiot I was.'

'A prize, yes,' Abby declared throatily, and lightly kissed his throat.

'Stop it,' he commanded, and his mouth quirked in self-derision as he continued, 'In my saner moments I told myself I was glad you had found someone else and were happily married with the child you so badly wanted.'

'Married?' she exclaimed.

'Yes. There was no end to my stupidity. You had gone to England on the same plane as Harkness.' He frowned as he said the other man's name. 'I concluded you had married him. It was only this summer, when an acquaintance of mine told me he'd seen a portrait of you in an art exhibition, and I couldn't resist going to see it, that I found out the truth. I asked the gallery owner if Harkness often painted his wife, and the man laughed and said the artist wasn't married, and he happened to know you were a divorcee and ran your own gallery down in St Ives. Once I realised you were still free, I determined to get you back. I told myself that if you had a child that needed a father, why not me?'

Listening to his explanation, Abby was filled with sadness at all the unnecessary pain and wasted years. She remembered her own anguish when he had disowned their child and she couldn't help asking, 'Did it never once occur to you that the child might be yours?'

He ran a hand over his eyes as if they hurt him. 'No,' he said tersely, 'and I'm ashamed to say it gets even worse.'

'Worse?'

'Yes. I hired a detective to check out the gallery owner's information. He confirmed you lived in St Ives and that there was no special man in your life, but he also gave me photographs he had taken of you. Jonathan was on one of them. Admittedly it wasn't very clear, but I should have noticed.'

'You hired a detective, but why didn't you just get in

touch with me?' she asked, unable to hide the doubt
clouding her green eyes. He had laid a very elaborate plot
to get her to marry him, and she could not still the niggling
doubt in her mind about his father's will.

'I was afraid.' He shrugged and smiled, but the smile did
not quite reach his eyes; instead, to Abby, he looked
heartbreakingly vulnerable. 'I didn't dare take the chance
of your refusing me. The detective told me about the
Trevlyn leisure project and it seemed the perfect excuse to
see you.' His expression hardened as he went on, 'But when
I arrived in Cornwall and found out you were engaged to
Trevlyn I was furious. I thought I was too late, and
Melanie's filling your head full of rubbish didn't help.'

Abby stiffened at the mention of the other woman, and
she inched slightly away from the warmth of Nick's body.
In her euphoria at Nick's declaration of love she had
forgotten about his other woman. Uneasily she wondered
if she would ever be able to trust him completely.

Nick reached one arm across her body and, curving a
large hand around her shoulder, he pulled her back against
his side. He gave her a sombre, almost angry glance.
'Melanie was my secretary, and never anything more,
though I admit I did once try to give you a different
impression. But that was purely for self-protection.'

She stirred restlessly in his hold. He had told her trust
was an integral part of any successful relationship, but he
had shattered hers once. Was she prepared to trust him
again? She still was not sure. 'Why *did* she stop being your
secretary?' The thought had been nagging her for days and
she had to know.

'Because she rang you and told you all those lies about
my father's will. I admit I did tell her I was going to ask
you to marry me again, but only because I was so happy
and I needed to tell someone. She had no right to interfere.'

'And were they lies?' Abby asked softly, not daring to
look at him, slightly ashamed at her lack of faith in him.

'Yes,' he responded angrily. 'My father gave me the
controlling interest in the firm over two years ago, and it's
in the company records if you need proof.'

Abby shivered at the icy edge in his tone and, seeing her reaction, he swept her into his arms, so they lay side by side and face to face. 'I'm sorry,' she murmured, 'it's just——'

'No, sweetheart, you're right. We need to get all the questions asked, all our fears out in the open. Perhaps if we had communicated more in the past, instead of spending all our time in bed, none of this would have happened. It was stupid of me to get angry.' He kissed her gently on the lips and smiled wryly. 'I did an excellent job of disillusioning you. Ask away, you're entitled.'

'I do believe you, Nick, but I seem to have got into the habit of always thinking the worst,' she confessed.

'I had noticed,' he teased, and it was her turn to smile wryly. He deserved to know the true extent of her cynicism, so she bravely told him.

'The day of your father's funeral, when we had almost got back together—well, I saw you in the study with Melanie. She had her arms around you.' And she went on to explain the conversation she had overheard.

'So that was why you rejected me,' Nick drawled. 'You read it all wrong. I had told Melanie you and I were back together and it was better than ever, and she was thanking me for transferring her to the New York office, because she had met an American tycoon and was getting married that week.'

Abby groaned at her own stupidity, and, looking into his smiling eyes, she knew she owed him it all. 'I have discovered that where you are concerned, my love,' she murmured huskily, 'I am an insanely jealous woman.' And she did not begrudge him his triumphant, purely masculine response.

'Good. I love it,' he declared arrogantly, a huge grin on his handsome face. But then, in a more serious tone, he added, 'God knows, I've suffered enough from the same affliction. I wanted to punch Trevlyn, and any man between eight and eighty who so much as looked at you.'

Abby chortled with delight, but was stunned to silence as he continued.

'And as for Harkness, I wanted to strangle him with my bare hands.'

'Oh, Nick, no,' she whispered, appalled at his anger.

'Yes, well . . .' He gave her a shamefaced smile. 'But the first time I walked into your gallery I was expecting to see a miniature Harkness, and when I saw Jonathan I couldn't believe it. He was a Kardis. I had to accept that, but it took a while to sink in. It was only as I was leaving that it finally hit me. He was mine, my son. For the first time in my life I thought I was going to faint. I spoke, but I don't remember what I said.'

Abby remembered how ill he had looked, and she knew he was telling her the truth.

'I couldn't accept the enormity of my mistake. I had missed my own son's birth and over three years of his life, and even more devastating was the knowledge that I had lost the woman I loved above everything, and all for nothing. It hurt, God, how it hurt!' he declared bitterly.

'It's all right now, Nick, darling,' Abby crooned, her hand moving delicately over his muscled chest in a gesture of comfort. Her long legs brushed his, the downy masculine hair arousing a tingling sensation on her flesh. She snuggled closer. Their hips met and she felt his taut power. 'Let's not talk.' She had another occupation in mind. Her hands roamed freely over Nick's body from shoulders to thigh, tentatively caressing his smoothly muscled contours, and then with more abandon she stroked the sensitive, tender places, and brought a deep-throated groan of delight from Nick's parted lips.

'Abby, I said later,' he gritted, and she gasped in surprise as suddenly he grasped her shoulders and rolled her under him. 'You're a witch woman,' he husked, his palms shaping her full breasts, and it was her turn to moan. Drawing back, Nick gazed down at the perfectly formed, hard-tipped creamy mounds, and Abby arched her body upwards in seductive invitation, wanting the intimacy of his caress. His long fingers closed over one hard nipple and rolled it gently between his thumb and forefinger. Abby sighed her pleasure, then sucked in her breath sharply as his fingers tightened almost painfully on her flesh.

'I think of you suckling our child, and I hate to think of any other man touching you like this,' Nick growled, and, lifting her eyes to his face, she was stunned by the fierce demand and underlying anger in their dark depths. 'Where you are concerned I find I am a traditional chauvinist and totally, unreasonably possessive.'

With a flash of insight, Abby realised that Nick's simmering anger of the past few months had been because she had allowed him to believe she had slept with other men. Quickly she tried to correct the false impression she had given him.

'There never was any other man, only you.'

His sensuous lips twisted in a wry grin. 'Thank you for that, Abby, but it doesn't matter any more. You are mine now, and I will never let you go again.'

He didn't believe her. 'But it's true, Nick. I was only engaged to Harry Trevlyn for one night.' And, stumbling over her words in her haste, she explained her relationship with Harry and Ian Harkness. 'You do believe me?' she asked.

'Of course I do, my darling.' And, as he lowered his head, his mouth covered hers, effectively stopping her garbled explanation. 'The future is ours,' he breathed against her mouth, and she parted her lips to accept the hot, moist invasion of his tongue. His throatily murmured words made Abby tremble inside. He was so right. They had a lifetime together to resolve any lingering insecurities.

Her tongue touched his and she felt the shuddering intensity of his response; his iron control broke at last. With a low groan his mouth dropped to find the hard peak his hands had teased to tautness only moments before. His fingers spread down over her flat stomach, searching and caressing, and he rediscovered all the erotic secret places he had known so well before. Abby writhed in silent pleading while her slender hands stroked down his broad back to his neat buttocks on a journey of discovery of their own.

With a growl deep in his throat he parted her thighs and

made her his in a wild, sweet coming together that was all the more poignant for their remembered lovemaking and the anguish that had followed. At last, their bodies and minds as one, they soared on a fiery trail to the heavens to be consumed in a mighty sunburst of passion that left them exhausted and satiated in each other's arms.

'The words have not been invented to describe how you make me feel,' Nick groaned, but with softly whispered Greek endearments he tried, as Abby lay entangled with him, her limbs heavy in the languorous aftermath of passion. He eased his weight away, but held her to his lean body, their entire lengths touching as though he would never let her go.

Gradually surfacing from the sensual haze that surrounded her, Abby had no more doubts. Nick was hers. She could feel it deep in her soul, and, dragging a long, shuddering breath into her oxygen-starved lungs, she finally came of age. 'The Doloreses of this world can do their worst,' she vowed.

'Dolores? What about her?' Nick asked in astonishment.

Abby turned scarlet; she had not realised she had spoken out loud. 'Nothing, I—I just wondered what happened to her.' To her chagrin she felt his mighty chest vibrate beneath her palm as he shook with silent laughter.

'Tut tut, my love, have you not made the connection yet?'

'Connection? What connection?' she pouted sulkily.

His silvery eyes, brimming with love and laughter, locked on to hers as he explained.

'Dolores Stakis is the widow of my friend Spiros, and Sophia Stakis is her daughter, my godchild, and they are both my friends—a responsibility in a way, but never anything more.'

She felt an utter fool, but a very relieved fool, and, flinging her arms around Nick's neck, she kissed him.

'Wait, Abby, there's something I want to do.' Pulling away, he slid his legs off the bed and stood up. Splendidly naked, he crossed the room and flung back the heavy screen that hid the jacuzzi, and, leaning over, turned on the tap.

Rejoining her on the bed, he lifted her over him so she lay spread-eagled on top of him, and grinning wickedly he said, 'How long do you think it will take? Five minutes?'

'You do mean the jacuzzi?' she teased, rubbing her breasts lightly against his muscular chest. 'Haven't you tried it?'

'No . . . I waited for you, my love.'

Later the cooling water lapped softly against her slender body as she lay in Nick's arms, deeply content. She gazed rather hazily up through the glass domed roof at the star-spangled black velvet sky. This was one erotic fantasy that surely worked, and she clung a little closer to her husband, a satisfied smile curving her love-swollen lips . . .

Abby sat before the roaring log fire in the living-room, a glass of mulled wine in her hand, waiting impatiently for her husband to come downstairs. It was Christmas Eve, and the past two weeks had been the happiest of her life. Nick had shed ten years overnight and was once more the vibrant, boyishly enthusiastic man she had fallen in love with so long ago. Their 'dream home' was a reality, echoing with love and laughter. A lightning trip to Cornwall had served to sign The Hope Gallery over to Iris, and assure her old friend of her happiness.

'God, let me out of this suit, I'm roasting,' Nick's voice drawled, and she looked up, her green eyes shimmering with laughter. No one could accuse him of not taking parenting seriously. He must have the only bespoke tailored Santa's outfit in Greece. She chuckled as he stripped down to his red boxer shorts, still sporting the white beard.

'Give me a drink, quickly, before I faint.'

Abby handed him her glass. 'What about the beard? It looks very authentic, but rather awkward for drinking,' she prompted.

Wincing, he ripped it off his face and held it out to her, a devilish gleam in his silvery eyes. 'It is authentic. Have you never heard of the Greek vendetta? We always get our revenge. It's goat hair. If not from my arch enemy, at least

a very close relative.' And, draining his glass, he placed it
on the mantelpiece with a triumphant grin. Abby dissolved
into fits of laughter, and finally when she could get her
breath she saw the opening she had been looking for all
evening. 'You really shouldn't harbour unkind thoughts,'
she remonstrated. 'The gynaecologist told me they can have
an adverse effect on our unborn daughter.'

'Our what?' he demanded, his eyes narrowed on her
flushed face, and she could sense the tension in his still
body.

'Well, it might not be a girl, but I am pregnant.' She
watched as a multitude of emotions chased across his
handsome features, from blank astonishment to a wary,
wondrous joy. Dropping to his knees at her feet, he clasped
her hands in his. 'Are you sure? Have you had a test?' Then
hesitantly, 'I thought you were taking the Pill.'

'Yes, yes, and no, I have never taken the Pill.' And,
freeing her hands, she slid her fingers through his black
curls, holding his head in her palms. 'I've told you
before—you are the one and only man in my life.'
Instinctively she had known he had never quite believed
her, but now, as his grey eyes, glistening with moisture,
blazed into hers, she knew he did . . .

Much later Abby was lying in the wide bed safely
wrapped in her husband's arms, almost asleep, when Nick
said, 'I think we should change our doctor.'

'I rather like old Popodopoulos,' she murmured
drowsily.

'"Old" being the operative word. He told me I was very
lucky to have fathered a child, and it was very unlikely to
happen again—something about a low count. I didn't tell
you because I had no intention of letting you go again.'

'Perhaps he's forgotten how to count,' she mumbled
stupidly.

'Well, if we do allow him to continue as our family
doctor,' Nick said seriously, 'it's essential we always get a
second opinion. Right?'

But Abby did not respond. She was sound asleep. Nick
smiled softly, and for hours he lay watching the woman in

his arms, thanking God, and every ancient god of Greece, for his good fortunes and second chances.

THIS JULY, HARLEQUIN OFFERS YOU THE PERFECT SUMMER READ!

Sunsational

**EMMA DARCY
EMMA GOLDRICK
PENNY JORDAN
CAROLE MORTIMER**

From top authors of Harlequin Presents comes HARLEQUIN SUNSATIONAL, a four-stories-in-one book with 768 pages of romantic reading.

Written by such prolific Harlequin authors as Emma Darcy, Emma Goldrick, Penny Jordan and Carole Mortimer, HARLEQUIN SUNSATIONAL is the perfect summer companion to take along to the beach, cottage, on your dream destination or just for reading at home in the warm sunshine!

Don't miss this unique reading opportunity.

Available wherever Harlequin books are sold.

SUN

Take 4 bestselling love stories FREE

Plus get a FREE surprise gift!

Back by Popular Demand

Janet Dailey
Americana

A romantic tour of America through fifty favorite Harlequin Presents® novels, each set in a different state researched by Janet and her husband, Bill. A journey of a lifetime in one cherished collection.

In June, don't miss the sultry states featured in:

Title # 9 - **FLORIDA**
Southern Nights
    #10 - **GEORGIA**
Night of the Cotillion

Available wherever
Harlequin books are sold.